And Hell Followed With Him

Chris Nardone

ISBN: 978-0-6152-1903-5

Prologue

Darkness.

An ominous chasm of death that seemed to taunt the young man.

The cowpoke sat next to his bedroll under the early morning sun on a flat, rocky ridge. His tall, gray horse was tethered to a clump of mesquite not five paces away, swishing its tail, nickering softly. The coals of his fire from the previous night had gone cold.

The young man sat deathly still for a few long moments, then brought up the six-gun he held in his hand. He gazed once again down into the depths of that black hole. The shadowy abyss from which death would explode.

The barrel of his forty-five Colt.

He should have realized long ago that he couldn't avoid this moment of fate. It was better this way. He'd brought nothing but pain and misery to all the folks he'd met. If he ended it right now, no one would know...or care. His corpse might be discovered, but more than likely, it would be devoured by the denizens of the desert.

The young man smiled.

He pressed the cold barrel of the pistol to his head, his thumb pulling back the hammer to half-cock. The clicking of the hammer mechanism sent prickles up and down his spine. Beads of sweat formed on his forehead.

He took a deep breath and cocked the hammer back fully. His index finger curled around the trigger, starting to squeeze it. Deep in the recesses of his brain, he could hear screams of agony, obviously some remnant of a long forgotten memory.

Pounding at his skull.

Taunting him.

In that instant before he pulled the trigger, he began to think about an unfulfilled duty to a dying friend...one of his only friends—to find the man who'd murdered him. He would never see it through now. Because he had to do this thing.

To end the misery---and greet eternal darkness with open arms.

The gun bellowed.

The young man turned his head, his ears ringing mightily, and saw his weapon pointing to the sky.

He couldn't do it. He couldn't end his life.

He wasn't quite sure what had stopped him, but he let the gun fall to his side, getting to his feet, moving past the tree branches and clumps of sage. He came to stand at the edge of the ridge, looking out over the desert valley.

He could see intermittent fields of green bordering an enclave of wind-blasted buildings. The young man sensed something was going to happen in that town. It was calling to him. An invisible force had reached out from the town, beckoning him to come. Why?

Here he sat on a rocky ridge, gun in hand, ready to end his suffering, but this feeling of being drawn was almost overwhelming. He walked back to his campsite, holstered his six-gun and began saddling his horse.

That was when he heard the heavy footfalls, and then a twig

snapping from somewhere in front of him. Glancing over the head of his gray, he saw the tall, stocky cowboy dressed in dusty chaps and cowhide vest step out from behind a cholla cactus.

"Did yuh think you could make a fool outta' me, Smelly Belly? Just ride on out and not expect me to come lookin' for yuh?" the man growled.

The cowpoke's eyes narrowed into sharp slits. "Mort, I don't know what you're thinking, but you best just ride back to the home ranch."

There was a demented gleam in Mort's eyes, and sweat poured from his chubby, whiskered face, his breaths coming in snorts that made him sound like a pig. He grunted and shook his head.

"I ain't gonna! You better slap leather, boy!"

The young man came out into the open about ten paces away from Mort, his hands falling near his side. "I guess it's a good day for you to die," he said with a touch of casual, cold menace.

The young man stood stock still—calm, cool and collected, while Mort was extremely agitated, clenching his fists near the gun on his right hip. There seemed to be a moment in time where all sound stopped, except for Mort's heavy, incessant growling.

The young man smelled death in the air, a hint of a sneer turning up one corner of his mouth. When Mort saw this, his eyes blazed and his hand went for his six-gun.

The cowpoke's gun leveled before Mort's had even cleared leather. Two shots roared from the young man's six-shooter, violently snapping Mort's head back in a red spray. The heavy body thudded to the ground in a cloud of dust. The cowpoke reloaded his gun, holstered it, and went about digging a shallow grave for Mort.

After the task was completed, he went back to saddling his horse, focusing his mind once more on the town that lay down in the valley. As he tightened the cinch on his mount, the young man stroked the gray's mane and gazed out beyond the hills where he now stood, remembering his thoughts before he was interrupted. "I've never felt like this, boy," he told the horse. "There's something down there. Whatever it is, I...need to be there. I can't explain it." Then he thought of something he'd read from Shakespeare a few years back. It seemed fitting at this very moment.

"'There's a divinity that shapes our ends, rough-hew them how we will'," he said softly.

With that, he pulled himself into the saddle and nudged the gray in its flanks, taking one last look behind him toward the heaped up rocks, sand and branches where poor old Mort would lie forever. He shook his head, not feeling much remorse for the dead bully, but touching the brim of his hat in bidding him farewell, whistling the tune of a sad ballad.

The young man named Bel Jensen rode on toward his destiny.

Chapter 1

The tall, dusty, blond-haired drifter known as Bel Jensen trotted his gray up to the old, weathered livery barn at the head of the main street. A lean, wiry hostler sat on a stool, working on mending a bridle when the horse and rider came in. He glanced at Jensen, taking in the man's solid build and his rugged features—a face tanned by the sun, a hawk-like nose and deep blue eyes.

Those cold eyes measured the hostler, and the man stood, took a few steps back, fumbling with the bridle, then setting it down on the stool. "Can I he'p ya, mister?" he stammered.

"Just want to put my horse up. Got room?"

The hostler looked nervously around to the stalls. "Uh, why, I 'spect we can handle him. You, um, stayin' long?"

"Don't know."

Bel Jensen paid the man and came back out into the morning sun, which was beating down hard now. He removed his Stetson, slapping the dust from his cowhide chaps and vest, mopping his brow with the bandana he kept tied around his neck. Replacing his hat, Jensen took stock of this town in the Arizona territory, which he discovered was called Dry Springs—the name was burned onto the side of the barn. The town was a single narrow street with about a dozen or so buildings on each side.

He saw a few small cottages dotting this end of Main Street, along with a few dry goods store, a clothing shop, a blacksmith, and the town bank. Further on at the far end of the street, Jensen guessed were the saloons, plus maybe a hotel or two.

Nothing seemed out of the ordinary, and now he wondered if that queasy feeling he got back on the ridge was a false alarm. He thought it would be a good idea to walk the town, maybe drop by one of the saloons.

The saloon, besides being a place to drink, was a clearinghouse for information. If he listened, and asked a discreet question or two, he might glean some useful tidbit that might help him in discovering what had thrust him into this seemingly peaceful town in the valley.

A door opened on his left, and he turned ever so slowly to see a woman exiting a yellow cottage with that fancy, so-called gingerbread trim. She wore a flowing, pine green calico dress with ruffles, folds, and lace trim but he couldn't see her face clearly.

Jensen also saw she carried a parasol in one hand, her other hand seeming to be amidst the folds of her dress. She came off the porch and extended the parasol, walking toward him. Stepping up onto the boardwalk, the lady turned to glimpse Jensen.

Giving him a glance, he could see a haunted look in her eyes. But, it lightened ever so slightly, and a hint of a smile flashed for an instant, then was gone.

She was a very attractive woman—prettier than those nudes he'd seen in many a saloon, with hair as red as copper. She looked to be in her late teens, had a slim, hour-glass figure, and possessed a pair of luminous green eyes that matched the flowers on her dress. That's when the feeling hit him like a hammer blow.

Now that he was among people again after being on the trail for a while, he knew that those dreaded sensations would once again bombard him. What baffled Jensen was that other images were creeping into his thoughts. Scenes that came with the suddenness of a photographer's flash bulb—a long stretch of wagons, thundering hooves with war-painted braves hooting and hollering war cries, the moans of sick people, and the grief of burying one's dead.

Bel Jensen twitched nervously to get the thoughts out of his head. What did they mean as he took in this beautiful young woman? She looked as though she noticed him staring strangely at her, and he had enough presence of mind to reach up and touch the brim of his hat to her in greeting. "Ma'am," he called out hoarsely.

She nodded to him, her face twisted with uncertainty. She continued on down the boardwalk, still giving him an occasional backward glance. His mind fixed on those pictures from his brain. In all his life, he didn't remember *it* ever happening like that.

It. That's how Jensen always thought of...IT. He couldn't understand or make sense of...those feelings. A gust of wind brought Jensen back to some semblance of what he called reality. He saw a rider coming up the alley in front of the red-haired woman. The rider brought his steed to a halt in front of the young woman on the boardwalk, then pulled a leg from a stirrup and hung it around the saddle horn.

"Howdy there, ma'am!" the young, pitted-faced rider greeted cheerfully. "It's a mighty nice day, ain't it?"

"Yes, it looks to be," she said, glancing up and down the street as if trying to locate someone.

"Whoa, wait! Where ya'll goin' in such an all-fired hurry?" the rider asked.

"Just up the street," the lady answered. "I'm meeting my father."

Bel Jensen watched the rider look around nervously, getting antsy, and then dismount from his horse. Jensen, although wary around most people because of their treatment of him, still had a deep, intense respect for women. Even if some of those women were the ones who taunted and belittled him. He believed it came from never knowing or having a mother of his own.

It didn't matter to Bel Jensen. Women were scarce in this country, and they were deserving of a man's respect. As far as he was concerned, if you harmed a lady or even spoke ill of her, you had hell to pay. So, when the young rider moved toward the young woman, Jensen felt a need to protect her.

But it was totally unnecessary. The rider held out his arm to her. "May I escort you across the street, ma'am?" he offered.

A brief smile adorned her features. Jensen could tell that for some reason, smiling, while it made her look radiant, was not something to which she was accustomed. "Thank you for your kind offer, sir, but I'll be just fine."

"Sure. Have a nice day, ma'am!"

When the pocked-faced rider climbed back into his saddle, Jensen thought it was quite odd. He guessed the man was waiting for some fellow cowpokes to meet up with him, but the rider seemed to have a burr under his bottom.

Why? Unless...the idea hit Bel Jensen like a runaway freight train. Maybe he was sitting his mount there for a reason. He had a clear view of the town bank diagonally across the street. A good place for a lookout to place himself and cover any escape out of town.

Jensen couldn't get a clear view of the bank from his position, but he thought he spied some horses tied up to the hitching rail out front.

"A bank robbery?" he breathed out loud.

Jensen took a few steps toward the rider. Now he felt it. He tried to wish it away, but it was no use. The rider became aware of his presence and turned to him. Bel knew what the rider saw chilled him to the bone.

Jensen stood completely rigid, his eyes glazed over...unfeeling, unwavering. They stared directly at the young rider. The cowboy couldn't stand it any longer. His face paled with fright, and his gaze turned from Jensen, for he seemed to spot something near him. "No, no!" he gasped.

The sound of gunshots interrupted the late morning stillness, and snapped Bel Jensen back to the here and now. The young rider also seemed to come out of his shock. "Shit! It's the boys!" the rider proclaimed.

"You're not going anywhere, pardner!" Jensen stated in a cold monotone. The rider focused on him, noticing his hand over the six-gun belted on his hip. The rider's face turned crimson with rage. "You son of a bitch!" he spat, fumbling for the gun on his own hip.

Jensen's draw was smooth and as quick as a cat, the Colt leveling on the rider. The cowpoke's gun was halfway out of its holster when Jensen triggered a shot that took the young man through the throat, exiting in a spout of blood, tumbling him from his saddle to land face-down in the dusty street. The horse, a tall roan, went bolting for parts unknown.

Bel looked around for the young woman, thinking he spotted her across the main street. But he couldn't worry about her now. His rugged features darkened as his deep blue eyes focused on the town bank. Suddenly, masked figures carrying what appeared to be heavy burlap sacks erupted from the bank. Bel Jensen felt frozen. Something was happening to him.

Bel's feet seemed nailed to the ground as they mounted their horses. Arms like quicksand, Bel couldn't even raise his gun to confront the robbers. He saw a grizzled old lawman across from the bank watching the bandits gallop away.

Why doesn't he stop them? Bel thought. The sheriff was snickering, and Jensen felt disgust overwhelm him. Or was it all his imagination? The sheriff was supposed to do his duty and stop these killers from getting away.

Then he saw it.

In front of the lawman was a huge rattler, about the size of a small wagon. It reared its head back to strike, exposing its dripping fangs. The sheriff's smile disappeared when he saw the giant serpent. He began to scream as the snake lashed out.

Bel's vision got cloudy. It couldn't be a dream, could it? The last thing he remembered were cries of terror emanating nearby and the thundering of hooves roaring past him. He thought he saw one of the outlaws raise his gun, firing off a round that went whizzing by his cheek, slamming into the building post behind him. But, Bel couldn't be sure, falling into a familiar darkness.

Chapter 2

The Past

A blinding flash of lightning.

A ground-shattering peal of thunder.

That's how it all started for Bel Jensen. At least, that's what he remembered. It may have sounded silly if he explained it to other folks, but he couldn't even be sure he came from a woman's loins.

All he knew were those two violent explosions of nature, and finding himself standing on the front porch of a large, two-story, wood-framed house during one of the worst rain storms that anyone could recall.

Later, he'd heard the storm referred to as an "apocalyptic deluge". But, there he stood on the porch in a neatly pressed gray suit with knee-high pants, alone and scared, not knowing how he had come to be there. At the time he didn't even know how old he was, but later figured he'd been about five or six.

The door opened a few minutes later and spilled out a glow of lamplight. Bel remembered seeing a tall woman wearing the habit of a nun. She had prominent cheek bones and lovely blue eyes, but hesitated before stepping out onto the porch. From inside, Bel heard a querulous voice call out, "Sister Katherine, get back in here out of the rain. You'll catch a death of cold!"

He saw Sister Katherine's face showing much compassion as she knelt in front of him, putting her hands on each of his shoulders. He started to back away, but then held his ground.

Bel noticed another nun framed in the doorway, this one short and squat, with a rough, wrinkled face and beady eyes. "It's okay, Sister Mary," Sister Katherine said. "He's just a...a boy. And...Holy Mary Mother of God! He's completely dry!" She crossed herself, and Bel noticed Sister Mary do the same. He saw Sister Katherine focus her gaze on him. "Are you alright, young man? What on earth are you doing out here in this terrible storm?"

Bel could only stare at her with a hypnotic gleam in his eyes.

"What's your name?" Sister Katherine asked.

Bel's mouth opened as if to answer, but nothing came out for a long moment. Then, he seemed to find his voice. "I...don't know."

Bel could see confusion on Sister Katherine's face. "You don't remember your name? Here, come inside where it's dry." She reached down to take one of his hands, smiling warmly. "Please, it's going to be okay."

Through the foyer, a stairway led to the second floor, while a front room branched off to the left. Past the stairwell and down a hallway was only shadows and darkness.

As she led Bel into the shadowy parlor of the house, he saw Sister Mary's eyes flare with suspicion. "What are you doing, bringing a strange child into this house? He has the look of the Devil in him, Sister Katherine!"

"That's absurd, Sister Mary," Sister Katherine said, obviously taken aback. "The boy is scared and..."

She touched his face, Bel expecting her to find his skin cold as ice, but it was warm to the touch. Her brow furrowed.

"Look at him," Sister Mary blared. "His clothes are not wet, and he's not even chilled! He's the spawn of Satan!"

"Ridiculous! He will stay here until we can decide what to do with him. And that will be that, Sister Mary."

Sister Mary sneered at Bel Jensen. "What are you, boy?" she growled. "Why have you come here?"

Bel seemed confused, looking down at the floor, nervously grinding his palms into fists. Sister Mary's eyes blazed as she kneeled in front of Bel, hissing, "Answer me, boy! Answer me!"

With tears welling up in his eyes, Bel gazed up at the two nuns. He didn't know why the words came to him, but he answered, startling them to their very core.

"I just am."

If he'd ever had a name before that dark, rainy night out on the frontier, he wished he could have remembered it. Instead, Sister Mary had been responsible for giving him his name. "You are a demon, Belial!" she had spat. "Yes...Belial Jensen. "It is a name for the devil, and a devil you are!"

Bel had found out later that for orphans, they chose surnames randomly. He had no problem with Jensen, but that first name...the name of some devil from the Holy Bible, well, only when he was older would he drop the "Belial" and answer to the name of "Bel".

Bel Jensen came to find out that the place wasn't an official orphanage. It was an old, but well-kept, double-spired adobe mission that sat on a grassy hill. It was run by a kindly old priest from town named Father Garcia.

The two nuns, Katherine and Mary came across the plains years ago from Independence, Missouri. While on the wagon train, Comanche's besieged it, and the few surviving members settled down in the valley below where the mission now stood. The folks called the town Sanctuary.

That fateful day, while war cries and arrows filled the sky, some children had become orphans, and the two sisters decided to care for those who had lost their parents. As the town grew and prospered, members of the town council ordained that construction begin on a proper house to shelter the orphaned children. So the townsfolk helped construct that two-story, wood-sided building that would stand next to the old mission.

There were never more than a dozen children there at a time, for that was all the nuns and the town could afford to house. Once in a while, a couple from Sanctuary would adopt a child and take them into their home. While at other times, a child might be found abandoned in town, so to the mission they were sent. Bel had heard those kinds of stories before, that parents not wanting children would abandon them. And it chilled him to his very core that people could be so cruel.

Life at the mission for Bel Jensen was tough and also cruel. Some aspects were no fault of the nuns and the townsfolk. Almost every night, Bel went to bed hungry, so he ate everything they put in front of him. Most of what the children got was by charity, courtesy of the town, whether it was food or clothes.

There was a parcel of farmland near the mission which allowed them to harvest fresh vegetables, but it was mostly slim pickings. If anyone misbehaved, they went to bed without a meal.

As life wore on for Bel Jensen, he discovered he never seemed to fit in with the other children. Teasing and harassment by the other mission children, as well as from children in the town became commonplace. The ones from Sanctuary would goad him about his poorly-fitting, hand-me-down clothing, or yell horrible things at him, because "he didn't have a mama".

The daily monotony of teaching Bel and the other kids about God, Jesus, and a dozen other saint and martyr names which he could never remember, and their larger-than-life exploits, grated on his patience. Bel would always sigh with irritation when forced to sit through the readings of the Good Book. No one was that all-powerful, Bel thought. They were just make-believe stories, he mused.

He could feel that Sister Mary directed all of her rants solely at him. Babbling about evil and how good would always prevail. What a bunch of horse crap!

This led to the boiling of Bel's temper at times, adding another mystery to his already strange life. During moments of intense duress, Bel would start to experience memory lapses. He caught one of the children asking Sister Katherine, "Sister, what is wrong with Belial? Is he sick or something?"

A deep frown adorned the nun's features as she replied, stroking the youngster's hair, "No, child. He's...well, Belial is unique, that's all."

Every time Bel regained his senses, someone around him was screaming or yelling in terror. Now and then, that particular child became catatonic and never recovered.

Two closely related events seemed to precede this new chapter in Bel's life. One hot afternoon found Bel taking a break from his daily chores and visiting some of the farm animals the orphanage kept. Bel loved interacting with the cows, horses, chickens and pigs. It was one of the few things he enjoyed doing at the orphanage. He knew animals were dependent on humans to take care of them. Sometimes they would shy away from him, but Bel understood the innocence they possessed. They would never yell at him or tease him or call him names.

Gentleness. It was a trait he wished people had more of.

Bel neared the pig pens and felt a touch of contentment as he watched the swine move about through the mud. One of the animals came lumbering over to the edge of the wooden pole fence. It stuck its snout through the opening, obviously hoping Bel was there to give him a meal.

"Sorry, big fella. Nothing for you today."

Bel heard footsteps behind him. "But you two deserve each other!" a voice cackled. "DEVIL! DEMON!"

Bel couldn't react fast enough as two older, bigger boys grabbed his arms and legs and tossed him over the top rail of the fence. He landed with a soft thud into the pit of slop. The pig snorted and squealed in defiance of having his territory breached. The animal, probably more scared than anything, pitched and wheeled on top of Bel. As he got to his feet, Bel saw the two boys running from the scene, their laughter echoing across the front yard.

Bel looked down at his ruined clothes with shame. He was filthy and smelled like pig shit. That was the moment when Sister Mary decided to come storming up to the scene, her wrinkled face twisted in anger.

"Belial Jensen!" Sister Mary growled. "You get your sorry self out of that pig pen and get cleaned up. Since you can't stay out of trouble, there will be no supper for you tonight!"

Bel didn't even offer a rebuttal. He knew it was pointless to explain to Sister Mary the truth about what had just happened.

Later that night as Bel trudged into his room to retire, he saw it was pitch black. Not wanting to wake some of the other children who had already turned in, he crept softly to where his bunk was. Having worked hard that day, Bel was exhausted. He nearly collapsed into his bed, but landed into a wet, squishy puddle. The strong smell of copper hit his nasal passages. It wasn't until he saw the feathered form next to his pillow, did Bel realize what was going on.

Someone had wrung a chicken's neck in Bel's bed and placed both the body and the head near his pillow. When Bel found himself covered in blood, he screamed in fright and despair, leaping off the bunk and waking the entire orphanage up.

Bel heard the taunting laughter. It was like acid in the pit of his stomach. It burned. Somehow, some way, he thought, those who teased him would be very, very sorry.

Bel struggled through the next several years as an outcast. He became more somber and was hesitant about trusting anyone. Sister

Katherine was always nice to him, but Bel figured because of his "episodes", she was struggling with any closeness to him.

He eavesdropped once on a conversation between Sister Katherine and Sister Mary. Coming down the staircase of the house, he spotted the two nuns below him in the main hallway off of the front room.

"We must talk, Sister Katherine," Sister Mary barked.

"Is it about Belial?"

Sister Mary's glare answered the question, and Sister Katherine folded her arms across her chest.

"Belial must leave this place!" the old nun complained.

"He's only a child, Sister Mary," Sister Katherine retorted.

"Three of the children will never be the same again, do you realize that?" Sister Mary said. "The longer he's allowed to stay here, the more he will curse this place with the shroud of Lucifer!"

"What does Doctor Williams say? Can he figure out if the children will ever come out of it?"

Sister Mary threw up her hands in despair. "He says he doesn't understand it. That demon, Belial went into some sort of fit, his eyes disappearing into his skull. Then the next thing anyone knew was that the children were thrashing around on the ground, screaming and hollering! It was so...awful!" Sister Mary took hold of Sister Katherine's hands in each of hers. "I know what he is, Sister Katherine! He's evil incarnate! Now those children just lay there, their eyes blank, staring off into space...mumbling incoherent things." She looked deep into Sister Katherine's eyes. "It's like...they're no longer human! They've fallen under His spell!"

Bel could only shake his head as Sister Katherine pulled away from Sister Mary, who seemed to be in a trance herself. "Stop it, Sister Mary! God forgive me, but I've heard what some of the children have done to torment Belial during his stay here. Two of them pushed him into the pig pen, calling him 'devil', and 'demon'. And those other two, one of the girls told me, put that dead chicken into his bed, just to play a trick on him. Belial has done nothing to deserve these things!" Sister Katherine stared daggers at her fellow sister. "I wonder where they might get ideas like those, Sister Mary? Could it possibly be that someone put those ideas into their heads?"

Bel could see Sister Mary was furious, even her eyes becoming angry. "How dare you accuse me!" The nun took a menacing step toward Sister Katherine, but after a long moment, it seemed that she was letting rage get the best of her. She stepped back, running a hand across her forehead, straightening her habit, and composing herself. She smiled at Sister Katherine, but it resembled a sneer more than anything to Bel.

"I apologize, Sister Katherine," Sister Mary said. "May the Lord forgive me for that outburst. I only want what's best for the children. If you remember, it was said in St. Matthew, 'beware of those which come in sheep's clothing, but inwardly they are ravening wolves'."

Sister Katherine closed her eyes, slowly shaking her head, crossing herself in frustration. "False prophets, Sister Mary!" she stated. "St. Matthew talked about false prophets! Belial isn't a prophet, he's only a child! And if YOU remember, it was Psalms that said, 'Children are an heritage of the LORD'. We have sworn by almighty God to take care of these children. Belial is one of those children, and he will stay here as long as he likes. I'm..."

"But Father Garcia..." Sister Mary interrupted.

"Father Garcia would come to me first if there was a problem with one of the children," Sister Katherine finished. "You have no right to decide this boy's fate, Sister Mary. Only He can. This conversation is over."

Without another word, Sister Katherine pushed past Sister Mary and strode out the front door.

Sitting on the back porch of the house, rocking back and forth on a swing that attached to the ceiling, Bel thought about the words he'd just heard. After hearing the two nuns talk about him, Bel felt an inkling of pride toward Sister Katherine for standing by him. He was glad at least one person didn't think of him as a beast. It was hard for him to comprehend those few blackouts he'd experienced.

When he'd come back to his senses and seen those children screaming their lungs out, thrashing about like snakes with their heads cut off, well, it had genuinely frightened him to his very core. And to find out later that he was somehow the cause of the ruckus? He'd heard the town doctor mention the word "seizure", but Bel wasn't sure what it meant.

On the other hand, Bel had to admit he didn't exactly feel any remorse for those who would torment him, just to get a laugh from the other children. No, Bel thought, it made him feel giddy when he thought of these...bullies getting their payback.

If only he could control these fits that he threw, then...a smile began to play across Bel's façade. One of the few smiles that he'd shown since he'd shown up at the mission. If only...

For a brief moment, his mind started to wander at the possibility of something he seemed to possess, but when the door banged open, he sank back into sullenness and continued rocking. That's when he saw Sister Katherine standing there, looking at him with curiosity, a tender smile on her kind face.

"May I swing with you?" she asked.

Bel didn't speak. He only nodded and made room for the nun on the swing. He watched as she sat down, then she reached back to undo the habit that covered her head. Underneath, he saw her short, auburn hair framing her gentle features. In all the time Bel Jensen had been there, he'd never once seen either of the nuns without their religious garb. For a brief moment, it made him feel kind of special, but then the moment passed.

"Don't you get tired of wearing that thing all the time?" he asked suddenly.

Sister Katherine chuckled. "It's one of the things required of us in our service to the Lord." She leaned forward and spoke softly to Bel. "But, to tell you the truth, it can be quite ridiculous! Don't let Sister Mary hear that."

Another smile swept across Bel's face for a brief moment, but then it turned stoic. "I...I heard Sister Mary and you talking. Am...I going to have to leave?"

Sister Katherine reached out to stroke Bel's blond hair, and surprisingly, he let her. "Oh, no," she said. "You aren't going anywhere...Bel. Do you mind if I call you Bel? It's much lovelier than that other name. It'll be our little secret, okay?"

Bel nodded. "Are they all afraid of me, because of...what happens sometimes?"

"They just don't understand you. Some people are afraid of things they don't understand." Sister Katherine's gaze tightened and became serious. "Tell me something, Bel. When you see these boys and girls who have tormented you again and again...suffering, does it make you feel glad that they are in pain?"

Bel couldn't help but look down at his hands, nervously twisting them into fists. When he glanced up at Katherine, he thought she was looking into his soul. "It scares me," Bel replied. "But, it serves them right for not leaving me be."

Sister Katherine nodded in understanding, reaching over to grip each of Bel's shoulders. "Bel, I want to tell you something, and I want you to listen carefully. Can you do that?"

He nodded and she continued. "Whatever gift you've been graced with, you must never give in to the horrible urges that might come with it. You may want to lash out against those who have wronged you so. But, when that thirst for vengeance fills every waking hour of every day of your life, it'll eat away at the good person I know you are, until there's nothing left but an empty shell—your soul, your very essence of being." Sister Katherine brushed a lock of hair from Bel's forehead. "Then you WOULD be that beast you were named for. Do you understand what I'm saying, Bel?"

"Yes, Sister Katherine," he replied sheepishly. Bel just sat there for a long moment, gazing at this woman of God who'd been the closest thing he'd had to a mother. Sitting here with Katherine, Bel

started feeling something within him. Not the strange feelings that left

him scared and confused. But...

Bel Jensen leaned over and wrapped his arms around the nun's

shoulders, hugging her gently, burying his face into her chest. And

he did something that no one in the mission had ever seen him do.

At least, not in their presence.

He began crying, holding Katherine even tighter. She welcomed

his embrace, stroking his hair ever gently, offering soothing words to

him.

"Don't ever leave me, Sister Katherine," Bel sobbed.

"I won't leave you, Bel Jensen," she assured him.

"You promise?"

"I promise."

Two weeks later, they replaced Sister Katherine at the Sanctuary

mission. No reason was ever given to the children. Just that she had

gone back east.

A young Bel Jensen was crushed.

Chapter 3

Bel Jensen came back to reality. Sitting in the dirt where he had fallen, he got a faint whiff of smoke, and heard screams fading away from his memory. A short, stocky man with thinning gray hair squatted before him, sunlight glinting brightly off the tin star pinned to his vest. Jensen saw a few curious bystanders looking in about ten feet behind the lawman.

The dream. It's happened again, Jensen thought. But he couldn't be too sure, as he took in the man. He had a mouthful of tobacco, making his jaw bulge. The lawman's dark eyes studied Jensen for a long minute.

"You should be more careful in town, stranger. I know folks said you plugged that desperado, but standin' out here in the street, plain as day, when a robbery is takin' place? What in blazes did you think you were doin'?"

The sheriff's harsh tone caused Jensen's eyes to narrow. "I just rode in."

"Then ride out."

"No, I think I'll stick around for a bit."

The sheriff shook his head in disgust. He stood up, hooking his thumbs in his gunbelt. "Name's Zeke Thompson. This is my town," he said, spitting a stream of tobacco juice only inches from Jensen's feet. Bel took that as a proverbial 'line in the sand' warning. "Best watch yourself, boy. Savvy?"

"I wish I did," Jensen muttered under his breath. He peered into the sheriff's eyes. The young man didn't like the lawman's tone one bit, and he could feel the stirrings of his temper wanting to flare up. He almost asked the man why he had his thumb up his ass during the holdup. But he kept that thought to himself. "What happened in there, sheriff?" Jensen asked coolly.

Thompson's gaze went down the street of false-fronted buildings toward the bank, and Jensen followed it, at the same time looking for the striking young woman he'd come across, hoping that she was alright amidst the morning's chaos. The sheriff's features hardened. "One of the bank clerks died," the lawman said.

Sensations that Bel had felt out on the trail crept into his mind. Could this be the reason he'd gotten that inexplicable pull toward the town of Dry Springs? He felt his composure slip. "Who did it?" he asked.

"Folks say it was Francis Collier and his gang of sidewinders," the sheriff replied, depositing another wad of tobacco juice on the dusty road.

"Francis Collier, the gunfighter?"

"Yep. He had Rance Welby, Dick James and Kid Merraux ridin' with him. Plus that feller you bagged who was coverin' their escape."

Jensen had heard of Collier before, known mainly for being a thief and rustler. Somehow, from the man's reputation, he didn't rate as a cold-blooded killer in Jensen's book. People do change though, he reflected.

The other names Jensen didn't recognize, but now Thompson eyed him strangely. "Why are you so interested in this all of a sudden?"

Jensen's eyes flashed with anger. "If you'd have done your job instead of shootin' the breeze, there wouldn't be this mess, would there?" Jensen bit off anything more, but was cursing himself inwardly for letting it out. The sheriff would probably kick his ass right out of town now, he figured.

The sheriff took one step back, shrugging his shoulders. "You're right, son. I missed the sign on this one. Now one of our own is dead, and I have to live with it." Thompson raised an eyebrow at Jensen, appearing concerned. Are you feelin' alright, mister? You ought to get that head looked at."

"I'm fine!"

But things were not fine. Jensen felt himself plunging into a dark, misty void.

SNAKE! KILL HIM! NOW!

The image of a hideous, coiled serpent screamed into his thoughts, and he tried to clear his head. Bel desperately wanted to kill this man. He wanted to reach over and rip out his throat. No! He thought of Sister Katherine's warning to him. He promised her, didn't he? But then again, she hadn't kept HER promise to him. He'd have to keep talking to settle himself down. "So, are you sending a posse out to get the Collier gang?"

Thompson nodded. "That we are, son. Would you like to join us?"

Bel could feel the sweat running down his cheeks, getting into his eyes, stinging profusely. "No."

The sheriff glared at Bel and frowned, his eyes narrowing. "See that you stay out of trouble then, stranger," Thompson said, and promptly walked off down the street.

SNAKE! KILL! DO IT NOW!

The image in Jensen's head faded as he watched the sheriff go. That was different, he thought. In his mind, it was like some malicious voice screaming at him. He was sure THAT had never happened before. Maybe coming to this town was not such a good idea, as the lawman now disappeared up the street.

Jensen took Thompson for a stubborn old fellow, but he had the notion that the sheriff was something else. Had the robbery surprised him, or did he allow it to happen? Why would the sheriff of a town be negligent on purpose?

He removed his Stetson, mopped his sweaty brow and tucked the hat back on his head. Bel Jensen felt himself calming down at last. He sat down on the boardwalk to take a breather, then saw a trio of townsfolk ushering someone from near the bank, across the street. When Jensen looked closer, at least two of the folk were women, along with one man. His gaze froze when he noticed it was the beautiful redhead he'd seen earlier that they were escorting. For a brief moment, he caught her eye as they passed him, and he could tell from where he sat, she'd been crying.

It took a few minutes for her to be ushered home to her Victorian cottage, and Jensen waited until the street was quiet once more. Then he got up, stretched, and ambled his way down Main Street.

What was he doing? Something had obviously happened to the young woman, and here he was, intending to intrude upon her grief? The Bel Jensen before today would have just walked back to his horse, mounted and rode off, not wanting to get involved in anything complicated.

As Jensen stood near the front porch of the cottage, he kept thinking this was for the pull towards the town of Dry Springs. He needed to stay his course and discover what was behind this immense, unseen magnet.

Making sure he looked presentable, straightening his vest, dusting off his pants, and removing his hat, he walked up the path to the porch and stepped heavily onto it, almost wanting the woman to know he was there.

Bel tapped the brass knocker three times, and could hear a body stirring inside. A few long moments later, the door opened, and the young man's heart fluttered as he took in the attractive lady once more. It hurt to see her pretty face now, flushed from crying, and her red-rimmed eyes, full of pain and sadness.

The stump where her right hand should have been took Bel off guard. That's why it had been tucked within the folds of her dress earlier. It took him a moment to find his voice, inhaling the intoxicating scent of her lilac perfume. "Howdy, ma'am," he said in a low, agreeable tone. "I don't mean to be a bother, as it seems like you may have just lost someone. And..."

Her gaze fixed on Bel's face as she spoke in a scratchy tongue. "I...I saw you speaking to Sheriff Thompson," she said. Clearing her throat, she continued, her tone clearer. "You're the man who killed the lookout for the robbers."

Bel's mind was a mess. He'd been glad she'd interrupted him, for he really didn't know what to say to this woman. All the girls he'd ever talked to made fun of him and teased him.

"Yes, ma'am," Bel answered. "It all looked mighty suspicious, then when the robbers came storming out of the bank, well..."

"You're not comfortable around people, are you?" she asked.

Damn, this woman was direct, Bel thought. Was he making that much of a fool of himself? He tried to answer her, but couldn't find the words. His mouth just hung open and he looked down at his boots. After a few pounding heartbeats, he found he could speak. "Beg pardon, ma'am, but you're right."

She cocked her head curiously at him, then turned from the threshold. "Would you like to come in?"

"Thank you."

Bel Jensen entered the foyer and saw a modest front room branching off to his right. Covering the walls was what looked to be cheap, but decorative wallpaper in a flowery print.

Below the front window was a cowhide settee, with a large, ornate Boston rocker next to it. A grandfather clock sat against the far wall to Bel's right, and a lovely portrait of a striking woman clad in an evening gown adorned the wall opposite the window. When Bel looked closer, he could see a resemblance between the woman who stood before him and the lady in the painting.

The room had a vaulted ceiling and an archway to the right of the portrait that led to the kitchen and dining room in the back of the house. Bel figured the bedrooms were on the opposite side of the cottage.

"Please, have a seat," she offered. "Would you like a cup of tea?"

"No, thank you," he answered. Bel sat down on the settee, and was quite surprised when the woman sat down next to him, rather closely, he noticed. His pulse started to race and he cursed himself inwardly. She won't bite, he reminded himself. Just calm down.

More sweet waves of her scent greeted him like a soft caress and it agitated him even more, setting off certain responses in his body that were uncontrollable. He felt himself grow hard.

The lovely woman tilted her head once more, gazing at him and Bel couldn't help feel like she knew everything about him, but that couldn't be true. "So, what can I do for you Mister...?"

"It's Jensen, ma'am. Bel Jensen," he stated nervously. "I was just wondering if there was anything I could do for YOU, ma'am."

"Were you going to help find my father's killers?" she asked. "Are you going to help Sheriff Thompson?"

"I'm not with Thompson," Bel replied. When she spoke those words, Bel's gut twisted with such intensity, seeing the desperation in the woman's face. Here was the source for her world crumbling today. He was not one to reach out to people physically, but this was one person whom he felt obligated to comfort. He paused, then did that which he wasn't accustomed to.

He put a hand on her shoulder.

"Your father was killed in the bank robbery?" Bel asked, already knowing what she would say.

She nodded slowly, chin trembling. "He never hurt anyone in his life," she said with lingering despair.

Inwardly Bel wondered why he'd waited so long, but he asked,

"What's your name?"

"Ella Desmond."

Bel cupped her chin and shuddered as he saw the pain in her fathomless emerald eyes. "You've had a hard life," he whispered, motioning toward her damaged limb.

"What?"

"When you were a little girl coming west on a wagon train? The Indian attacks. The Cholera. The death of your mother." Bel glanced up at the painting on the wall opposite him. "That's her, isn't it?" His eyes narrowed as he studied the portrait for a moment, then gazed at Ella once more, his eyes filled with compassion.

Ella leaned away from Bel, astonishment taking over. "Who are you?"

His mind became a swirling mass of distorted images. Bel couldn't quite fixate on anything concrete, unlike what he'd seen of the sheriff. "You're strong, I can see that," he said. "You have nothing to be afraid of."

"Who are you?" she repeated.

"I'm nobody," Bel said.

Ella got to her feet quickly and went to stand under the portrait of her mother. Wiping her eyes, she looked at Bel with cool determination. "I'd like you to leave now, Mr. Jensen."

Once again, his curse had shot him down. Speaking the words he did, it was like he'd been in a trance and couldn't stop himself. Now, this beautiful lady who had no one left was asking him to go. Bel simply nodded, got up and replaced his hat, touching the brim. "I'm very sorry to have disturbed you, Miss Desmond." He walked to the front door and opened it.

Without turning around, he said, "'Suffering is permanent, obscure and dark, and shares the nature of infinity.'" Bel paused for a few seconds, then continued. "You know, this morning when I woke up, I didn't plan on ever seeing another sunrise again. I've had too much pain and misery in my life. It was just eating away at me, gnawing at me like some old buzzard. And then, for some reason that I can't understand, I was drawn to the bluff, looking down at this little town. It looked so peaceful. Some unseen force was telling me that something was going to happen today. That's why I stopped from blowing my brains out. I thought, maybe by coming here, I'll be shown the path to a brighter future. That's all drifters ever want...to do something worthwhile, to have something to look forward to. To have a place that they can call...home."

Bel turned and stared directly at Ella Desmond. "And I won't get that until I help you. That's why I was brought here today, Ella. I know that now." He touched the brim of his hat one more time and turned to walk away.

"Wait!"

Bel swung around and saw Ella coming to him, stopping only inches from his form. "I think," she said, sniffling, wiping her nose, "that it takes great courage to endure all that you have, and to face what life throws at you, day after day. My father once told me that you have to face your fears...and conquer them."

Ella reached up with her left hand and touched Bel's face. He inhaled her lilac perfume and closed his eyes, laying his hand over hers. Then he opened his eyes, and their gazes met. "It may not mean anything to you, Bel," Desmond began, "but I always remember a line by Marcus Aurelius that said, 'Nothing happens to anybody which he is not fitted by nature to bear.'

"You ARE strong, too, Bel Jensen. I wish you luck on wherever your journey takes you." She kissed him softly on the cheek and brought him into an embrace. Bel's eyes stung as he accepted the beautiful woman into his arms. He was shocked that a girl would want to touch him like this. He just wanted to stay like this forever, holding this young lady close to him, and to never let go. But, he did as his breath came in quivering gasps.

"Thank you, ma'am," is all he could say.

"Please forgive me for my outburst. You'll always be welcome here, Bel," Desmond said.

Then Bel was out the door and heading back down the street toward his horse. He was compelled now to help Ella Desmond. The only thing was, he wasn't a tracker or lawman. Where would he start? He'd figure that out soon enough, he thought. Bel Jensen stood in the street for a few moments, his features tightening. Then he turned and strode off.

Ella Desmond watched the mysterious young man leave her father's house. No, that's not right, she thought. It's MY house now.

Ella wanted to go to her bedroom and let all of her pain out. Just remember father's words, she scolded herself. I have to be strong, too, she thought. She had all sorts of feelings coursing through her at this very moment. Aside from all the grief, her chest swelled with pride at what this young man meant to do for her. How long had it been since she'd put her arms around a man...other than her father giving her a hug and kiss goodnight? Too long, she thought.

Most men shied away from her when they discovered she was "damaged". But this Bel Jensen had made an indelible impression on her, even though she misunderstood his presence there and wanted him to leave at first. She could feel deep down his intentions to help her were honorable and sincere. It wasn't like some men whose eyes would roam up and down her body, most likely with one thought on their minds. She didn't get that from Bel. No, he was gentle and compassionate if one got to know him, she guessed. A tortured soul, definitely. She sensed a coldness about him, a grim determination that would see him run roughshod over any of the monsters who would stand in his way of...helping her.

Bel Jensen would risk his life for someone he barely knew. And wouldn't expect any sort of reward for his effort. He was doing this deed for *her*.

Her.

That thought alone moved her beyond words. Her breast ached with desire. She wanted Bel to be safe. She wanted him to return...to her. Ella couldn't help feeling how much she wanted to put her arms around his strong shoulders again. God, she so dearly wanted to touch his stubbled cheek once more. To kiss him more deeply than she'd done just now. If she could gaze lovingly into his eyes, maybe he'd be able to see into her heart...her very soul and her being.

"Just come back, Bel Jensen," Ella whispered. "Please come back."

Ella went to the window, spotted Bel guiding his horse past her house and heading out of town. A curious thought occurred to Ella Desmond as she watched the young rider gallop on down the street. It was from the Holy Bible, Revelations.

"'And I looked, and behold a pale horse; and his name that sat on

him was Death'," Ella recited, watching Bel Jensen disappear from view...

"'And Hell followed with him.'"

Chapter 4

The Past

Bel Jensen sank back into sullenness and retreated within himself after the departure of Sister Katherine. He didn't eat much, and spent many days confining himself to his bedroom, not wanting to have contact with a single soul.

He didn't really blame Sister Katherine for abandoning him. Bel always figured Sister Mary had something to do with it. He would inquire politely now and again as to why Sister Katherine had left, but was either ignored or another subject was brought up.

Sister Katherine's replacement was a plain Hispanic woman with a wide mouth and many crooked white teeth. Her name was Sister Guadalupe. Or Sister Lupe as the children came to know her. She was polite but stern to Bel, even though he was sure Sister Mary gave her an earful about the "demon in him". In fact, it was Sister Lupe who was responsible for bringing Bel out of his current slumber.

A few days after her arrival, Bel lay curled up in his bed, the covers over his head. His head buried in the soft feather pillow, he cried softly, wishing, praying for Sister Katherine to come back. When all of a sudden, there was a loud crash and Bel jumped up from the bed.

Standing there was Sister Lupe holding a mop, and a tin pail at her feet where she'd intentionally dropped it to make the maximum amount of noise. "You will clean this floor, Belial," she ordered. Without another word, she strode off.

Bel didn't know what to do. He felt like lying back down and ignoring the chore. But, Bel always did what the sisters told him to do. He was never defiant, and certainly not a troublemaker. Only in the eyes of Sister Mary, he concluded. It took him a few minutes, but eventually Bel got to his feet and proceeded to mop the floor.

That was the beginning of his return to the daily grind of living at the mission. There was still the teasing and goading now and then, but Bel made himself a promise. He would use work to occupy his time and to try to put his feelings about Sister Katherine's departure in the back of his mind.

Not that he didn't already have chores to do. The children at the mission all had duties they were assigned. The older ones had the more physical jobs to do—chopping wood, plowing the fields, or scrubbing walls, floors and dishes. The younger ones mainly helped the sisters or Father Garcia.

As the adolescent years approached Bel Jensen, his physique had grown from the puny boy that he used to be, to a lean, muscular young man. Being bigger than most of the orphans at the mission, the constant prodding dropped off considerably. He still kept to himself, and Sister Mary's demeanor never changed toward him, but he found himself going into town more, and getting away from the mission.

It was on a cool, sunny spring day that would find Bel Jensen entering another phase of his life. He'd been in Sanctuary where he'd work every now and then for one of the shopkeepers, opening boxes and stocking shelves with supplies.

Deciding to take a short break, he walked down the dusty main street of town, with a work apron tied around his waist, a hammer dangling from a loop. Bel moved toward an eatery where he'd been promised all the hot, black coffee he could gulp down for his hard work.

He exited the café with the scalding cup of brew, leaning on the awning post, taking in the refreshing breeze that had started up. That was when he noticed an unshaven character dressed in buckskins standing about five paces away in the street, gun at his side, eyes focused and determined.

Bel saw the tall, stalwart man coming up the street, a man whose face showed signs of being hardened by the outdoors. Looking to be in his mid to late thirties, he had slits for eyes and a strong, stubbled jaw. The man was clad in black, broadcloth trousers and a black checkered shirt and cowhide vest, and Bel glimpsed the tin star pinned to his chest. He also saw the marshal wearing two tied-down sixguns.

Then the buckskinned stranger spoke, aiming his sixgun. "You killed my brother, Marshal! Now I aim to kill you!"

The marshal stopped, his hands resting on his gunbelt. He shrugged his shoulders. "Well, Boyd, if that's what you came here to do, you might as well have at it." Then his voice dropped a decibel, and its tone came from the grave. "But you'll die, too."

"What? You're crazy! I got the drop on you, lawman! Are you saying that I'll miss?"

The Marshal was calm and cool. "You might get me, Boyd, but I'll definitely get you."

"You think you're that fast?"

"Fast enough. You can't win, Boyd. So why don't you just turn around and ride out, and we'll forget all about it?"

Through this exchange, Bel saw movement in the upper window of the building next to the marshal. A rifle barrel emerged from the window and Bel saw the muzzle dip toward the lawman. The young man couldn't believe this was happening. He was about to see a real live gunfight, but felt he had to do something or else the marshal was going to be hurt.

"Look out Marshal," Bel shouted. "Second floor window!"

Everything started to happen at once. Boyd was taken by

surprise and snapped his head to see who'd shouted to warn the lawman. He sighted down his six-shooter and was thumbing back the hammer when Bel dropped his coffee cup and took up the hammer from the loop on the apron he wore, slinging it at the badman with all his might.

The object slammed into Boyd's wrist just as his gun boomed, spoiling his aim and jarring the weapon out of his grasp. The slug kicked up dirt a few feet away from the marshal.

At the same time that was going on, the marshal heard Bel's warning and whipped both his guns out of the holster, his left-hand gun aiming for the second-floor window. The lawman's pistol barked three times, the rounds smacking through the pane of glass just as the rifle boomed.

The .44 round whistled over the marshal's head, but the lawman knew his shots had been placed perfectly. The gunman crashed through the glass, tumbling across the building overhang, hitting the dust with a thud.

Boyd was cursing, holding his hand in pain, glaring at Bel who stood behind the building post, which didn't offer much cover, but standing fast nonetheless. The outlaw saw his pistol a few feet from where he stood, the marshal coming forward with both his guns aimed.

"I wouldn't do that, Boyd," the lawman warned. "It's all over."

What happened next perplexed Bel, for he seemed to see a shimmering, like heat waves in front of Boyd. The strange mass started to take on an indistinct shape, but Boyd's eyes focused on the configuration, and they bulged out in complete terror. No one else seemed to notice it.

"NOOOOOOOOOO!" he bellowed at the top of his lungs, grabbing for the gun.

"Damn it, Boyd!" the marshal shouted.

The buckskinned man just had a grip on his gun when the lawman's two sixguns bellowed out their lethal response. Boyd's chest rippled a spray of crimson as the slugs took him high in the torso, spinning him around, pitching him to the dust.

The marshal came running up to the downed man, keeping his guns trained on him until he was sure he was dead. Some townsfolk had gathered, and the lawman waved them back. "Go back to your business. It's all over here!"

Bel still stood there behind the building post, trying to decipher this latest event which he knew had to do with his curse. That roiling mass that he'd spotted. He'd gone a while now where he hadn't been bothered with anything out of the ordinary. Now he was faced with this latest mystery. The marshal interrupted his thoughts. The man walked up to him and held out his hand.

"Appreciate the warning, son," the lawman said. "Didn't realize Boyd had someone else with him."

"It's quite all right, Marshal," Bel replied, accepting the man's hand.

"You from 'round here?" the marshal asked.

"I live at the mission."

"I see." The marshal smiled broadly. "By the way, I'm Micah MacLean."

"Bel Jensen."

"Well, maybe I'll see you around?"

"Yeah, maybe."

* * *

The next day Bel was busy chopping wood for the stove out in front of the house when he saw a rider coming up the hill from town. When the figure got closer, he saw it was Marshal MacLean riding a big roan and he was leading a tall gray horse. Bel was hot and sweaty and he dropped the ax, wiping his brow, getting embarrassed when he eyed his worn-out trousers and ripped shirt. MacLean kicked up a cloud of dust as he reined in his horses.

The door smacked open behind Bel and he turned to see Sister Mary hurrying down the steps to greet the marshal. "Why, hello, Marshal," she greeted in her kindest voice. "What brings you out here? Is there something wrong?"

"Good morning, Sister Mary," MacLean answered, touching the brim of his hat. "No, I was just wondering if Bel here wanted to take a ride with me. Uh, that is, after he's finished with his chores."

Sister Mary frowned, giving Bel a nasty glare. "Bel won't be able to, I'm..."

"It's alright, Marshal," a voice came from the house. Moments later, Sister Lupe came out to join everyone. "I think Belial has done enough for this morning." She turned to Bel. "Why don't you go get yourself cleaned up? That is, if you want to take a ride with the marshal?"

Bel felt his pulse jump. He wouldn't mind getting away from the mission and Sister Mary once more. "Thank you, Sister Lupe. Marshal MacLean, I think I will." MacLean nodded, and Bel's eyes gave Sister Mary a dismissive glance, then he was hurrying inside.

Sister Mary walked up to the marshal. "Marshal, you shouldn't bother yourself with Belial. He's...well, he's not right."

MacLean frowned. "Why on earth would you say something like that, Sister?"

"Just heed my warning, Marshal!"

"Oh, hush, Sister Mary," Sister Lupe scolded good-naturedly.

Sister Mary turned her nose up and walked away with a snort. Marshal MacLean couldn't help but chuckle to himself.

Ten minutes later, Bel came back out dressed in worn wool pants more presentable than the ones previously, and a red-checked shirt with a hole in the elbow.

"Got this nice gray for you, Bel, and he's rarin' to go," the marshal said.

"I don't ride much, Marshal MacLean," Bel told him.

"Not to worry, son," MacLean replied. "We'll have you ridin' like an Injun soon enough." He turned to Sister Lupe. "What time should I have him back, Sister?"

"Supper time would be good. Thank you, Marshal."

Turning their mounts, Bel was the first to see the dark figure at the far end of the hill. He couldn't be sure, but he thought the character was dressed in some sort of cloak. And if he wasn't mistaken, he was holding a long stick of some kind. But the figure was too far away to be absolutely sure. Then Marshal MacLean's eyes fell to the dark figure and Bel saw the man's facial muscles twitch.

"What the..." MacLean breathed.

MacLean looked to Bel to make sure he'd seen the figure too, but when he looked back to the edge of the hill, there was nothing there.

"Marshal, are you...?" Bel began to ask.

"Sure, son. I'm fine. Let's get a move on, huh?"

They galloped away in a cloud of dust.

Chapter 5

The Past

Bel didn't realize it when he and MacLean rode away from the mission that he was going to get a surprise. But, Micah MacLean led the way into town and they pulled up rein in front of a clothing shop. When Bel emerged from the store a little later, he was wearing a brand new pair of trousers, a starched, red-checkered long-sleeved shirt, a cowhide vest, a black, flat-crowned Stetson, and shiny new boots.

They were off again, riding out of town and heading into wild country. The pair galloped through dry stream beds, skirted a few hills and came into a rocky canyon with steep, towering walls of granite that loomed over the two riders like giant sentinels.

"I can't thank you enough, Marshal," Bel said. "I've never gotten a gift from anyone before. These clothes are something I'll never forget. Especially after what I've been wearing after all these years."

"Well, son," MacLean said. "I owed you. I just wanted to show my thanks."

"I'll never forget it."

Bel noticed Marshal MacLean looking at him for a moment, his brow furrowing in thought. Then the lawman asked, "Say, what was that all about back at the mission? Sister Mary called you Belial? Isn't that from the Bible?"

Bel nodded. "That was the name I was given by Sister Mary," Bel explained. "She has this crazy idea that I'm the devil's spawn or something."

MacLean burst out laughing. "Well, I'll be a hog's butt! That's a good one, that is. Ah, don't let it beat you down, son. Them religious types can get some really fool notions inside their heads."

As the sounds of the horses hooves clacked loudly and echoed inside the canyon, Bel wondered where the lawman was taking him. Then they came into a clearing where the limestone walls weren't that steep and Bel could see some tin cans laying around in front of the stone facing. Marshal MacLean brought his horse to a halt and Bel did likewise.

Dismounting, MacLean went to the pile of cans and began setting them up. Bel started to get some idea of what he was going to be doing and it filled him with a sense of excitement.

"You ever fired a gun before, Bel?" MacLean asked.

"No, not yet," Bel replied.

"Well," MacLean said, "I think every young man needs to learn how to shoot. Good time as any to start. What do you think? Up to it?"

"I have a feeling that the nuns wouldn't approve," Bel said.

"Let me tell you something, son. A gun can be a very dangerous object. In the hands of a man with bad intentions, it can be deadly. As you saw the other day with Boyd." Marshal MacLean walked to his roan and dug inside his saddle bag. He brought out a gunbelt and holster, inside of which was a Colt Peacemaker. "But, a gun is also a tool. A very important tool. Just like an ax or a hammer or a broom. When you're out here in wild country, you use it to stay alive. You get me?"

"Yes, Marshal."

"I use it only when it's absolutely necessary," MacLean explained. "Believe me, Bel, I don't enjoy killin', even though some folks may think that it comes easy to a man like myself. It don't." Then he looked Bel straight in the eye, taking hold of the gun he held by its grip. The snapping sound it made as MacLean jerked the pistol from the holster made Bel flinch. "But, when this comes out of the holster, all bets are off. If you're facing down another man, it's either you or him. If you don't think faster than him, you're dead. Just remember, getting off a shot first doesn't mean a thing. It's where you put that first shot." He gave Bel a crooked smile. "Let's just hope you don't ever find out what that's like, son."

Micah MacLean turned the gun around butt-first and offered it to Bel. "Do you wanna give her a try?"

"Yeah, I'd like that."

For the rest of the afternoon, Bel practiced with the sixgun, hitting most of what he aimed at. Marshal MacLean would give instruction to Bel, and correct him now and again if need be. Bel discovered that his reflexes were incredibly good at times, something he attributed to his heightened senses of everything around him. That damn curse, he thought. That's what it was.

It was a perfectly happy day, Bel reflected. But, the worst was yet to come.

For the next several months, Bel Jensen spent more and more time with Marshal Micah MacLean, sometimes even staying the night at the marshal's house on the outskirts of Sanctuary. MacLean taught Bel how to ride, how to hunt, and how to live out in the dry, arid wasteland known as the desert. In short, he taught the young man how to survive.

MacLean also showed Bel the ropes in the business of ranching, should Bel ever want to go that route in his life—the marshal told him he'd spent plenty of time as a cowhand in his youth.

But mostly, Bel rode out to the canyon and practiced with the sixgun MacLean had given him. Of course he had thoughts about wearing it, but he knew the nuns at the mission would never allow it. He also thought about wearing the gun around town, too.

With wearing a gun comes great responsibility. One was being careful what he said to another man in the West, for the rules were different out on the frontier than they were back east. You didn't call a man names and expect to get away with it without a shooting.

So, Bel decided he wouldn't wear it...yet.

Bel also found out more about Micah MacLean's past. He'd been a cowhand, had ridden as a shotgun rider for Wells Fargo, and had been a deputy sheriff. When he would talk about the love of his life, Sally, Bel always noticed a grim expression overcome the marshal.

One night, the rain was coming down in sheets as Marshal MacLean sat in his office, a small, cramped, square cubicle with a rifle rack on one wall, and a wooden, roll-top desk on the other. Beyond the front room was a metal cage that led to the jail cells.

In a corner opposite the marshal's desk was a small table that would belong to a deputy had the marshal needed one. Bel sat there, busy cleaning his gun, listening to the steady plop-plop of rain leaking through the roof and splashing into strategically placed buckets throughout the marshal's office. He noticed MacLean was preparing to make a patrol of the town before retiring.

"Micah, do you mind if I ask you something?" Bel ventured.

"Sure, son," MacLean replied. "What's on your mind?"

"What happened with Sally? How'd she die?"

That same haunted look overcame the lawman. He gave Bel a steady gaze, dropping his feet from the desk to the floor, leaning forward in his chair. "Well, you know Sally died ten years ago," MacLean said. The lawman paused for a long minute. "She died giving birth to our son."

That was it. He'd said it. Abrupt and final.

Bel's stomach turned to mush, and he felt sorry for his friend. But, he also understood. Understood the pain of losing someone special.

"What about...?"

"Our son died right after she did."

Bel thought that Micah was breaking down when he spoke those words, but he couldn't tell.

"I guess it's as they say," MacLean said. "The Lord does work in mysterious ways." The marshal gave a bit of a chuckle and shook his head. "I've tried to understand why they were taken from me, but I guess I'll never understand His ways."

"I know what you mean, Micah," Bel agreed. "I always wonder why I was put here on this earth. And wonder if I can make a difference."

"Well, if we talk about this stuff any longer," MacLean said, "we might get it in our heads to go on a bender."

That was how Micah was. Whenever someone started prying, he always had to change the subject. Bel didn't mind, though. He'd just been curious. He'd told the lawman things here and there about his hard childhood and his "curse". But, he didn't tell him everything, and he'd respected MacLean for not pushing things. He would give Micah the same consideration.

"I think it's time to walk the town one last time tonight," MacLean announced. "Wanna join me in this downpour?"

"How about I walk with you to the edge of town? Then I'll just head up the hill to the mission?"

"Sounds good to me." MacLean got up from his chair and strode back toward the cells, looking up toward the ceiling. He grimaced as he saw a few of the pails were nearly full of water. "Guess I'd better empty these before we leave."

"Here, I'll give you a hand, Micah," Bel offered.

"Naw, it'll only take a second."

Bel put his cleaning tools away in the desk, getting up and stretching his tired, aching body. He watched MacLean go out the back door and toss away one bucket of rain water.

But, as the lawman came back inside from the raging storm, Bel thought he saw something standing in the doorway. It was a dark shadow, but when Bel focused in closer, he thought it looked like the apparition that he'd seen that day MacLean had come out to the mission.

It was an eerie, cloaked figure which had no discernable facial features, and he carried some long stick-like object in his hand. Bel couldn't tell what it was. The marshal was bending over to pick up another bucket, and didn't see the shape. Bel's mouth opened to shout some kind of warning, but nothing came out. His heart started to pound wildly, with Bel croaking out a feeble grunt.

When Maclean turned to go out, Bel was unnerved when he saw the doorway was empty. What was going on with him, Bel wondered.

Bel leaned over the small desk he'd been using to calm himself down, but then heard voices coming from outside the back door of the marshal's office. Over the heavy rumble of the storm, Bel couldn't make out what was being said.

"Marshal?" he called out.

Bel walked past the grating into the cell area, but found his steps slow and methodical, as if sensing something was terribly wrong. Then he heard snippets of MacLean arguing with someone.

"....You're drunk! Go on, get out of here, mister!" he heard MacLean shout.

Bel heard what sounded like scuffling, then two gunshots that could be heard above the downpour. The young man started to run.

"Micah!"

Bel burst out the back door into the wind and rain, seeing Micah MacLean in a sitting position against the wall of the outhouse which was attached to the office proper.

"God, no!" Bel wailed.

MacLean was holding hands to his bloody stomach, his gun lying in the mud only a few feet away. His head tilted up to glance at Bel as if he was in some sort of trance. Bel was in a similar state of shock as he sank to his knees in the mud, at Maclean's side, hoping he could do something for the wounded man.

There was a splash of footsteps and Bel saw a hurried movement out of the corner of his eye. He turned to see a looming figure, feeling something slam into the side of his skull. He pitched forward next to MacLean, his head spinning wildly from the blow.

Whoever it was stood there for a moment in the raging storm, looking down at the two helpless people. The only thing Bel saw was a blur as he tried to clear his jumbled head, hearing the figure speak. It was indistinct, and the man sounded like he was intoxicated. But, Bel would never forget when the figure said, "'Now is the end come upon thee, and I will send mine anger upon thee...'".

The young man waited for the bullet to slam into him and turn his world black, but it never came, never hearing the retreating footsteps. Instead, the rain continued to pelt Bel and his friend as they lay in the mud.

Bel's head throbbed, but he was able to get once more to his knees and grip Micah MacLean by the shoulders, shaking him, praying that he was still alive. Hope leaped into Bel's eyes as MacLean's eyes opened, but he was fixated on something over Bel's shoulder.

Oh, no, Bel thought. Their assailant was coming back. But, when Bel slowly turned his head, he got a horrifying glimpse as to what the marshal was seeing.

Standing before them, like a mythical giant, was a cloaked figure. A figure with no face, only a black abyss. In the giant's skeletal hand, he held a scythe.

It was Death.

Micah MacLean began choking, his eyes bulging out, obviously able to see the creature. "Oh, God!" MacLean wheezed. "No, not me!" he gurgled, blood bubbling from his lips. Bel was petrified, unable to move a muscle in his entire body. When he saw Death raise his scythe, he tried to protect Micah's body, throwing himself in front of the dying marshal.

Then, Bel blinked and there was no one. He looked to his friend, and saw that he was dead. Bel gritted his teeth and cried out in anguish, his body heaving, his breath snorting like some wild animal.

Bel punched at the ground, wails of pain exploding from his throat with each resounding thud into the wet, slimy mud. Then he got to his feet and took one last look at the soaked and bloody body of Micah MacLean.

This was the last straw, Bel thought. He couldn't stay here any longer. It was time for him to move on, away from the mission and away from everyone else. Bel had no choice now. The strain of losing everyone he got close to was too much for him to bear.

He needed time alone, away from civilization.

Bel staggered off, wandering aimlessly through the town before he got his gray, packed up a few belongings from Micah MacLean's house, finally making it back to the mission.

Chapter 6

Bel Jensen's memory was always quite hazy when thinking about his departure from the mission. He lit out that very same night of MacLean's killing, riding off for parts unknown.

The next several years found him drifting from place to place. Sometimes he would camp out in the wilderness for days on end, while other times would find him going into town for supplies. He didn't want to get too comfortable with town life, though.

As the months passed, he would take on a job here and there. Bel realized he couldn't avoid people forever, and he was going to have to try and get some sort of steady employment. He needed money. And he would do it the legal way, by working for it.

He took on some riding jobs, punching cows and driving them to market. Bel always kept to himself during those times, never striking up any friendships. He did more than his share of the work and was loyal to all his employers. Bel remembered that Micah would call that "riding for the brand".

During his time as a cowpuncher, Bel would be the one to stay back at the ranch in his bunk, reading a book by Shakespeare or Sir Walter Scott, while the other ranch hands would go to town for a barn dance or a night of drinking in the saloon.

As long as his fellow punchers respected his privacy and weren't a bother, Bel was content. Every now and then though, he'd get a few barbs thrown his way by cowhands with chips on their shoulders, out trying to prove something to the other men, and it rankled Bel to no ends.

The last one would drive Bel nearly over the edge. He was out on the grassy range with the other ranch hands hunting up the strays from the herd. Bel worked hard, the boys knew that, and they wouldn't think about harassing him when doing the job. Crack lively jokes and tell stories, sure.

But Bel was a top hand, he carried his own weight when working, and was greatly appreciated by all. Except by the ranch owner's nephew, Mort. The tall, stocky man nearly got them in trouble with his inflated ego and bragging ways.

Bel had seen some riders earlier on the horizon that were not from the ranch. He was dead certain of that. They would appear ever so briefly, disappear behind some trees or rocks, then appear again.

Bel figured out what their plan was, keeping his gray a good distance away as to not attract attention.

They were rustlers, and they looked to steal some of his boss's stock. Bel had to find some of the other hands so they could chase these low-down thieves off.

Bel came over a grassy knoll and saw some of his cohorts up ahead clustered near a rocky ridge, with large outcroppings of stone. Bel didn't know if the boys had confronted the rustlers, but he dismounted from his gray, starting to make the rest of the way on foot to see what was up.

Bel cat-footed his way up the low incline, taking cover behind a large boulder. Peering around rock, he saw Mort and two other ranch hands that'd stopped to converse with four men. Bel got a brief glimpse of the would-be thieves. They were rough-looking, all with unshaved features, scraggy, narrow eyes and mouths that were etched into thin, rigid lines.

Their leader sported a jagged scar from his right eye down to his chin. Bel noticed Mort was trying to act tough with the fellow.

"Well, now," Mort announced, "what have we here, boys? I think we might have ourselves some rustlers!"

Scar-face gave Mort a deranged glare. When he spoke, his voice was harsh and scratchy. "I'd rein in that mouth of yours, piss ant! We were doin' nothin' of the kind, were we boys? See, some of our cows happened to get away from the rest of the herd. We thought they might have come up into these rocks here."

"You know who owns this ranch, mister?" Mort asked. "He doesn't take too kindly to stock thieves. If'n we figgered to hang you boys, we'd be well within our rights!" Mort chuckled to give Scar-face and his bunch a scare, but the men with Mort were visibly nervous, and these hardcases didn't frighten that easily.

Scar-face pulled the flap from his linen duster to expose the sixgun on his hip. He leaned forward in his saddle, the silence being so acute, the riders with Mort could hear the creak of saddle leather.

"Now, boy," Scar-face hissed, "I already told you why we was up here. If I were to get riled and think you were calling me a liar, I reckon I'd have to take this pistol here and use it. What do you think about that?"

Mort was also wearing a gun, as did most cowpokes out on the range, but he swallowed hard and was noticeably sweating. And by the aura these men gave off, the last thing he wanted to do was draw and get himself killed. He just didn't want to look bad in front of the boys.

"Uh...now look...m-mister," Mort stammered, "I'm n-not ca...calling you a liar. I just think that we should..."

"You think we should take our cows and head on out, do yuh? Well, that's exactly what we were plannin' to do, ain't that right, boys?"

Bel, from behind the rocks heard the rustlers chuckling and knew for sure that these men were going to be taking stock that didn't belong to them. Scar-face was banking on the fact that this braggart speaking to him was all hot air and wasn't going to lift a finger to stop them. Plus using the subtle threat of that gun on hip would cause any man to refrain from rushing into something.

Bel could feel the roiling in his brain beginning as he came from around the rock and walked brazenly out into the open near his cohorts.

As if there was a drastic change in temperature, a shadowy pall of dread seemed to invade the clearing. Scar-face and his men got one look at Bel, their composures slipping into a terrific case of the shivers.

"There a problem here, boys?" Bel asked with his usual low-toned menace.

Scar-face couldn't seem to get his tongue, for he stuttered and stammered over trying to explain why he and his low-down snakes were on range that didn't belong to them.

"Good," Bel said with finality. "Now you damn, no-good rustlers can turn those mounts around and stay off this range. Otherwise, next time you see us, there's gonna be a shootin'. Understand?"

"We...uh...I think we g-get your point, mister!" Scar-face stuttered. "Sorry for the misunderstandin'."

"And leave the cows where they are," Bel reminded them.

As the four riders turned to gallop away, Mort's transformation was amazing. He held up his fist at the retreating horsemen. "And don't come back, yuh hear?" he shouted. Then he turned to face the other two men, giving Bel a sneer. "See that, boys? They wasn't gonna mess with us while I was here!"

Nobody said a word as they gathered up the stray cows and headed them back to the home ranch. Bel then broke the silence.

"You boys head on in. I'll hang back to make sure our friends don't have a change of heart," he said.

"Yeah, whatever," Mort sighed. "You do that, Smelly Belly!"

Later on that day, Mort couldn't stop boasting to his uncle and the other boys about how he had single-handedly run off a bunch of rustlers. Some of the hands were loafing outside the corral in the main ranch yard near Bel.

"That's right, boys! I ain't afraid of anything or anybody!" the nephew declared arrogantly. "Did you see those yellow-bellies turn tail?"

"'O what a tangled web we weave, when first we practice to deceive'."

The cowhands turned to look at Bel, who was sitting on the top rail of the corral. Mort sneered. "What did you say, Belly Boy? You quotin' some lines from that Shakespeare feller, callin' me a liar?"

Bel's cold eyes bored into the other man's, shaking his head at Mort's lack of understanding a line from Sir Walter Scott. "Everybody has something deep down that they don't want to let out," Bel said. "It's as simple as that."

The bully snorted. "Well, I surely ain't afraid of you, Belly Nelly!" He took three large strides toward Bel, shoving him violently from his perch, laughing as the young man tumbled back and landed in a cloud of dust. Mort chortled, "You ain't even worth a pot of piss!"

Bel lay there for a few moments wincing in pain. Then his vision clouded over.

When he awakened, Mort was screeching and flailing like a madman. "Get it away from me! Get it away from me!" the troublemaker had screamed. It took four of the other cowhands to get him under control.

Bel tried to explain to his foreman that he didn't do anything. The ramrod had listened, but his mind was made up. "I'm sorry, son. That boy may be a tad unfriendly, but he's the boss' nephew. He's in such a frightful state, I don't rightly know if he'll ever recover." He put a hand on Bel's shoulder. "You've earned your wages, but I think this would be a good time for you to move on."

Bel didn't argue. He packed up his things and rode out...mentally exhausted from the years of abuse, fed up with this curse he'd been saddled with.

Bel began to entertain thoughts of just putting himself out of his misery once and for all. What Bel wouldn't find out until much later was that a few days after their run in with Scar-face and his rabble, the ranch hands would once again be back up in that rock formation hunting strays.

They would come across the most grisly sight any of them had ever seen. Four men staked out in the sun naked, with their heads scalped and strips of their skin peeled from their bodies. And thousands of ants devouring what was left of the carcasses.

Just like an Indian would do.

A week later, Bel Jensen found himself on that ridge, gun in hand, ready to end his life...

Chapter 7

Francis Collier was not a happy man.

As the four riders continued pushing their horses southeast from Dry Springs, Collier, the thin, hook-nosed, gaunt-featured outlaw who led his gang to the bank in that sleepy enclave fumed over their situation.

It was supposed to have been an easy job. Go in, get the money and ride out with minimal resistance or trouble. But it all went to hell when Dick James had decided to plug that poor bank teller.

Francis Collier, a southern gentleman from Georgia, had lost his home when the Yankees stormed in during the late unpleasantness and burned everything to the ground. He'd killed a Union soldier during a scuffle in a saloon, fleeing west to avoid prosecution.

In the years since the war, he'd acquired gun skills as he traveled, dabbling in petty crimes, finally moving up to stealing. From ranch payrolls to rustling to stagecoaches, he'd eventually graduated up to the most common form of thievery: bank robbery.

Collier, notorious for having killed eight men in fair fights, wasn't a bad man at heart. He loved to have money, not by working for it, but by taking the short route—stealing it, which made for the least amount of effort and work. But, he never would kill a man in cold blood, or shoot him in the back. If he had to kill a man during a job, he figured it was justified.

But that bank clerk back in Dry Springs hadn't been doing anything to provoke the outlaws. He was giving them the money just as he'd been ordered. It was that damned Dick James, who for no reason that Collier could see, just sighted down the barrel of his Smith and Wesson .44 Russian and put a couple of slugs into the teller's face.

Collier looked over to James, the hairy giant of a man, long greasy hair with thick, unkempt beard and mustache; the perfect frame for the savagery that lay beneath. James never seemed to be in a good mood. He had cruel eyes and was easy to agitate. Even though James always kept to himself, Collier somehow knew that he'd left a lot of corpses in his wake. Who knew how many dance hall girls he'd mauled and beaten, along with the many unlucky saddle tramps he'd shot in the back. The outlaw knew James was a pure-bred killer of the lowest order.

Collier should have never let the man talk him into hitting that bank in Dry Springs. But it was James, who had shackled up with Collier a few years back, always having some job in mind. And those jobs had paid off handsomely. That was the only reason Collier kept the man around. The outlaw leader figured he could take the brutal man in a fight, but as long as he was proving useful...

"Somethin' botherin' you, Francis?" James asked, his voice low and deadly.

"I'd like to know why you went off half-cocked back at the bank!" Collier said in his southern twang. "There was no reason to kill that man. You nearly got us into a fix, and you got poor Jeb killed."

"You worry too much," James growled, sticking his finger into his ear and working his jaw as if he was plugged up. "Besides, that teller was lookin' at me funny. I didn't like it."

Collier knew James had some sort of ear problem, and the outlaw figured the man deserved whatever discomfort he was experiencing. Francis smiled inwardly.

Collier thought about the youngster Jeb. It had been his first job, but he had a tendency to let his mind wander. He'd failed at covering their escape, and the outlaw wondered if it had to do with a skirt. Yeah, that was probably it. Jeb and the Kid had fast become friends, but they thought about women too much. This time, it had cost Jeb.

"Francis is right. You shouldn't have killed that teller, Mr. James," Rance Welby said, his mount falling in behind Collier's. Welby was dressed as a dandy, being clean-cut and handsome, clad in a navy blue coat, a fancy silk vest and blue pants.

He was a distant cousin to Francis Collier, and Collier knew he'd been a small town preacher years back. But, stealing from the weekly collection, and having angry townsfolk breathing down his neck, wanting his blood, forced the man to drift west.

Welby had a penchant for gambling and drinking as evidenced by the crimson sheen that adorned his facial features. He'd gotten out of more than one scrape at a card table, not by using his gun, but by his natural gift for talking. When he had to use his pearl-handled Colt, along with the sleeve gun derringer, his aim could be dead on.

"I'm afraid you're going to go to Hell, Mr. James," Welby stated matter-of-factly.

James scowled and smiled at the same time. "How many times do I have to tell you, Welby, there ain't no Hell!"

Welby looked up toward the heavens and closed his eyes, fingering the cruxifix that hung around his neck. "'Oh my God, relying on Thy almighty power and infinite mercy and promises, I hope to obtain pardon for my sins' and uh, for the sins of my companions, 'the help of Thy grace, and life everlasting...'"

"You shut your bazoo, boy!" James blared. "I'm getting' tired of listenin' to your bible crap!" To emphasize this, James once again was rubbing his ear methodically.

"Enough," Collier said, "Both of you!"

The last rider, Kid Merraux, spoke up from the rear of the pack. "Hey, Fran! Where we headin'?"

Merraux was a young man of about eighteen, scrawny, short and baby-faced with a shock of curly blond hair. Collier knew the Kid had once come west with the Orphan Trains. But, getting into trouble on many occasions, he'd run away from the family he'd been placed with.

He'd tried to steal Collier's horse, and had been caught. The outlaw could have plugged him right then and there, for killing a horse thief was considered 'justifiable homicide' in some places.

No, Collier had taken the boy in and schooled him in the art of stealing. He'd used the Kid many times as a diversion for stopping a stage or robbing a payroll.

Collier was still lost in his thoughts when James' booming voice interrupted him. "Yeah, Francis. The runt wants to know what we're doing."

Merraux was about to offer a retort, but Collier answered. "We're heading to the hideout," Collier said.

"What about the posse that's sure to be breathing down our neck?" Welby asked.

"Don't worry about the posse," Collier answered, not willing to give his gang too much information about his plans.

"When are we gonna split up the money?" James wanted to know.

"We'll do it at the hideout," Collier said sternly.

Collier brought his mount to a halt with a pull of the reins, and his cohorts did likewise. The outlaw leader turned to look at his gang.

The area of the country they were in was a shrub desert. Although there were occasional patches of grass, the trail ahead of them was ripe with yucca, agaves and Creosote bushes.

It was extremely hot in this part of the territory, and the riders took the time to wipe the sweat and dust from their faces and mop their brows with bandanas. "We're going to split up," Collier announced. "Rance and I will continue on to the hideout. Dick and Kid, you two will go your separate ways."

James and Merraux were about to offer their complaints, but Collier held up a hand. "Look, I've spent a lot of time thinking this through. Splitting up and giving the posse more than one trail to follow will help our chances. We've outrun posses before and we'll do it again."

"I don't like it, Francis," James growled. "Are you sayin' you ain't forkin' over the money till we get to the hideout?"

"That's what I'm saying, Dick," Collier said. "If you don't like it, you can always light a shuck and get nothing."

"Why you..."

James' hand dropped to his gun, but in a blink of an eye he was staring straight into the muzzle of Collier's pistol. "What's it going to be, Dick?"

The big outlaw seemed to be thinking it over, wondering if he could drag iron and get Collier before he himself got tagged. He knew it was useless. The hairy man gave a big, toothy grin, taking his hand slowly off the butt of his gun.

"Okay, Francis," James conceded. "We'll do it your way. But, know this. We'll have this conversation again when we get to the end of the line."

"Fair enough," Collier said, holstering his own sixgun. "Dick, just do your thing. Hole up somewhere, stay out of sight, whatever. Just give it a few days, then high-tail it to the hideout and you'll get your share of the money."

"What about me, Fran?" Merraux asked. "I know of this mining camp where..."

"No!" Collier snapped. "Stay away from towns. You'll just kick up a row."

"Okay. Speaking of trouble, Fran," Merraux said, "you don't think they'd send Will Dundee after us, would they?"

"I doubt it, Kid," Collier said. "Don't get your spurs all twisted."

Collier remembered back to an incident in Laredo. The Kid had been causing a ruckus in one of the saloons, and Will Dundee happened to be passing through. Dundee had a reputation as a marshal and town-tamer in the west. He'd been involved in many gunfights and was plenty tough.

During that rowdy evening, Dundee put the Kid over his knee and slapped his bottom blue, then took him by the ear and tossed him through the bat-wing doors, depositing him to the dusty street. The lawman told him if he ever interrupted a drink again, he'd take the Kid out to the desert and stake him down like an Injun would, and leave him for the ants and the buzzards.

When the Kid came to, he'd pissed and shit his drawers, taking the threat seriously, and high-tailing it out of Laredo. When Kid told Collier about it, the outlaw leader laughed, figuring the lawman was joking. The incident scarred Merraux for life, having fits of terror at the mention of the name Will Dundee.

"Remember, Kid," Collier cautioned, "I know you and Jeb liked to have a good hoo-rah together, painting the towns and such, but not this time. You got a lot of money coming to you, so don't blow it. Understand?"

Merraux's mind was working, but he wasn't looking at his mentor. "Sure, Fran. I get it."

"And no dippin' your little nub into some piece of calico," James called out with a laugh. "Yeah, we know where your head is at!"

Kid Merraux blushed at the remark, a sly grin on his face. Collier held out his hand to the Kid, and Merraux took it. "Good luck, Kid," Collier said. "See you soon."

With a rebel yell, Kid Merraux put spurs to his horse and he was galloping off in a cloud of dust. Then Collier saw Dick James wincing in pain, massaging his ear as he got ready to ride off.

"Are you ill, Mr. James?" Welby finally asked.

"I'll be fine, damn it! Just have my cut ready when I get there."

"Oh, don't worry, Dick," Collier assured him with a wink. "Just don't keel over on the trail, hear?"

"Not likely!"

Then he was off into a gallop, disappearing into the heat waves on the horizon. Collier and Welby kicked their horses into a trot.

"Something's bothering you, Rance. What is it?"

"I had a dream last night, Francis," Welby said solemnly.

"What about?"

When the sharply dressed man looked over to Collier, it sort of gave the outlaw leader a bit of a chill. "Mr. James chided me about the existence of Hell. I do believe there is one, Francis. I think we will know Hell and damnation in all its fiery form unless we turn ourselves in."

"Comon, Rance! You don't believe all that fire and brimstone stuff, do you?"

Welby had a blank stare on his face, turning to eye Collier. "I dreamt that the devil himself came for me, Francis. It all seemed so real. But there he was. Cloven-hoofed, forked tail, an ugly horned face. I'll never forget that vision as long as I live. I...I just think it might be time for me to repent."

Collier became silent for the next few minutes, for he thought about his own nightmares, those terrifying visions that haunted him almost nightly. He didn't know why those horrid, blood-curdling images came to him while he slept. He'd known them ever since he was a boy. Best not dwell on ghost stories and such, he thought. Collier turned to Welby.

"Look, Rance," Collier said. "When we get to the hideout, everything will be fine. We'll have money in our pockets, and you can do anything you want."

Welby sported a thin smile, worry etched into his face. "Do you still plan on getting rid of Mr. James once and for all?"

"I'm afraid so. 'The Man' says it has to be this way. Plus, that's more money for us."

"And the Kid?"

"I don't know. I do have feelings for the boy, having had a hand in raising him. But, we'll just see what 'The Man' wants to do. If he says to plant the boy six feet under, well...I don't know what I'll do."

"Let's hope," Welby stated, "that the good Lord will see it in His divine wisdom to not plant us six feet under...before we can enjoy the fruits of our labor, eh?"

"Amen to that," Collier said.

The two riders continued on their journey, never realizing that vengeance was not far behind.

Chapter 8

Three hours out of town, Bel Jensen saw the smoke billowing in the distance. It didn't look like any sort of Indian signal. Bel guessed he was too far north of hostile country for that. No, there were other dangerous denizens at work here. But, something substantial was going up in flames.

He'd left Dry Springs soon after his visit with Ella Desmond. On the trail as he ate some jerked beef from his saddle bag, his mind filled with soothing thoughts of the lady's kindness toward him.

His chest had swelled with an aching desire toward Ella, something he had rarely experienced in all his life. That incredible feeling was what drove him now. He'd hunt down the vermin who took Ella's father away from her.

As Bel came over the ridge, he saw the small log cabin set in a stand of mesquite trees smoldering, with a large pole corral next to it in shambles. Pieces of the fence were broken and smashed, and whatever horses had been there before, were now gone.

Most of them, that is.

When Bel put spurs to his horse and rode closer, he saw the carcasses of at least three horses lying amidst the rubble. Bel could hear the unmistakable drone of flies buzzing over the dead animals, and looked up in the sky to see the buzzards starting to circle.

It looked like it had been a stage stop. But, whoever had hit it had blown through the place like a tornado—quick and merciless.

Even though the desert was blasting out heat like a furnace, Bel felt slightly chilled from surveying the carnage. Again, there were no signs that renegade Indians had done this—no arrows, no lances, nothing.

Bel pulled up rein at the edge of the broken corral fence and swung down from the saddle, his eyes scanning the property carefully. With one deft move, his sixgun was in his grasp.

All's that could be heard at this point was the crackling and popping of wood from the burning cabin, and an occasional cawing from the buzzards circling above, waiting patiently for the opportunity to feast.

Bel crept forward toward the front porch of the cabin, his eyes once again focusing on the dead horses. That was when the pungent smell of death and decay assaulted him. Bel's nose twitched and he pulled the bandana from around his neck to cover his face and lessen the odor.

No, there was a person lying amid the horse carcasses. That's what he'd seen. Bel raced over and saw the horribly blackened figure sprawled out next to his horses.

"Christ!" Bel swore. "What kind of animal would do something like this?"

Bel took the corpse by his arms and pulled him out of the corral and laid him gently by the front porch of the cabin. The stench of burned flesh was still hanging in the hot, dry air as Bel kneeled down to examine the dead man.

From what he could tell, the gent had been in his thirties, possibly early forties, thin build and balding with a hard, wrinkled face—no stranger to this country. That face, in death, however was now etched in eternal agony. Bel realized the man didn't die quickly.

One side of his face was scorched and raw, laced with angry red pustules. Then Bel saw the man's hands, blackened by fire, two of the fingers on his left hand, apparently burned clean off.

So, the man, whom Bel decided was the stationmaster had been tortured.

Suddenly, a terrifying cacophony of screams blasted Bel's eardrums, and at the same time, a grim, ghostly visage seemingly appeared in the air above the dead man. A visage of a blackened, rotted figure, reaching out with a skeletal-like hand, flesh dripping off the limb, beckoning him from beyond this realm.

"I come for you, gringo!" the thing hissed.

Bel let out a yelp of surprise, rearing back onto his rump, thrusting his gun out to ward off the horrid specter. But everything was as it was a few moments ago—the burned out cabin, the dead horses, the dead man and the hungry buzzards above.

Bel stood and walked back to his horse to calm himself, thinking of who could be the perpetrator of this foul deed. One of the Collier gang? He was betting on it. It was too much of a coincidence.

Wiping his brow with his bandana, Bel decided to look inside of what was left of the cabin when he heard it. No, it wasn't a scream from beyond, or a buzzard call, but something else. Something...human.

Moaning. Someone moaning in pain. At first, the noise was indistinct, but when Bel backed himself up against the weathered front side of the cabin, it sounded like it was coming from around back.

With his gun leading the way, Bel took each step with care as he rounded the side of the smoldering cabin. The moaning was getting louder. And it sounded like that of a woman. Bel's head began to pound.

"Oh, God, no!" he gasped.

He approached the corner of the house, willing himself to go forth and see what the source of this terrible moaning was. Bel peered around the edge of the cabin and saw the woman sprawled out; her face was in the mud just off the bottom step of the porch. The rest of her body was lying across the steps and porch.

Her clothes, what looked to be a gingham dress was in tatters, her long auburn hair trussed and matted. Holstering his gun, Bel came to her and cradled her in his arms, very gently turning her over.

She looked to have been pretty once, but her prominent cheek bones were now black and blue, smeared with streaks of dirt and blood, her right eye swollen shut. Bel also noticed that her one arm was dangling uselessly at her side.

With pent up fury boiling inside him, Bel, as with the stationmaster, could guess what had happened to the woman. And it sickened him. An unwritten law of the West toward women had been broken. His entire chest was burning with rage.

But, there was something else, as he studied the woman, whose eyes were slowly coming into focus on Bel's face.

The woman reminded him of his long lost friend, Sister Katherine, and he was finding it hard not to imagine that this was the kindly nun he was cradling in his arms.

"Ma'am," he said in a low, gentle voice, "who did this to you?"

Her eyes seemed to flit from side to side, as if she was searching her ravaged brain for an answer. Then they focused once again on Bel. "Big...man," she croaked weakly. "Hairy...disgusting."

He had to give the lady credit with the agony she was experiencing, to be able to convey that much of a description. He smiled at her, trying to make her feel at ease. "Ma'am, I have to get you to the nearest town. You need a doctor."

A painful spasm wracked the woman's body. Then she shuddered, which sent little prickles up and down Bel's spine.

The woman was dying and she knew it.

He could see her eyes pleading with him, her mouth trying to form some last words. "Man...called himself...James."

Then the tears were flowing from Bel's eyes and he started to say, "No, no, no" over and over again.

Bel was still thinking of Sister Katherine's abandonment of him years back and he sobbed, "No, Sister Katherine, don't go!"

He brought the woman to him, holding her as lovingly as he could, just rocking back and forth. It was a few moments later when Bel felt the woman go limp in his arms. He laid her down gently on the porch and noticed the peaceful look she now had on her face. He leaned over and kissed her softly on the forehead. Then Bel suddenly realized he didn't know either of their names. He thought about going into the house and looking for something that might give him an idea of their identities. But decided he didn't want to know.

Now he never would.

Bel Jensen spent the next half hour burying the stationmaster and his wife. When he'd finished, he found a plank of wood and put it at the head of the two graves, then wrote on it, "Murdered by a coward".

Going back to his horse, Bel prepared to leave this once peaceful home. A home turned into a slaughterhouse by sick, twisted individuals with no conscience. Bel got back into the saddle, was thinking about the woman's last words.

He stared out beyond the hills, letting the white-hot rage boil inside of him. The person responsible for this would pay dearly. And he knew who that person was.

"Dick James," Bel uttered, "You son of a bitch! You are so dead!

You're gonna die screaming!"

Bel kicked his horse into a trot and headed out into the desert once more.

Chapter 9

It was early evening when Bel Jensen reached the outskirts of the small mining camp called Hollins. Set near the outlying slopes of the Dos Cabezos, the place consisted of two saloons, a hotel, livery, general store, and what was euphemistically referred to as Portia's Pleasure Palace.

But, as Bel saw the mining camp in the distance, he started to hear an eerie whispering inside his skull. It sounded like supernatural voices, guiding him to this settlement. Bel realized with the utmost dread, that it was his special power enshrouding him once more.

It had been a long exhausting day, what with the gruesome discovery at the stage stop, coupled with the long ride across rugged terrain. As darkness fell across the country, the desert air came with a chill to it. Jensen felt uncharacteristically tired, and he had to keep himself from nodding off.

Bel tried to keep his eyes open as his gray trotted onto the main street of Hollins. He didn't see too many folks about. Down at the far end of the street, he heard hooting and hollering coming from the saloons, along with a piano playing a rag.

Bel figured he'd walk the town before hitting the local drinking establishments. If he didn't fall out of the saddle first, he thought. When he closed his eyes for a moment, Bel could see a roiling black cloud that began to take on shapes.

He heard laughing and giggling.

The shapes became a young man and a scantily clad woman, rolling around in a bed. When Bel opened his eyes, he stared directly across the street at the two-story, wood-framed hotel.

Then he was falling...down into a mysterious shadow world. In that instant, the dark void enveloped him.

* * *

Kid Merraux and the scantily-clad woman on his arm laughed and giggled as they staggered up the stairs of the two-story frame hotel. Merraux held a bottle of whiskey in his other hand, taking generous swigs of the liquid, his free hand fondling and groping the whore's assets.

Calling herself Lila, the lady of ill repute was somewhere in her thirties, with blond hair and rough features that weren't softened by the layer of rouge she'd spread across her heavily lined face. She also had a nasty knife scar spread across her cheekbone that turned the young man off.

But, the Kid wasn't about to be choosy on this night. And besides, the little burg didn't have much else to offer in terms of woman-flesh.

"Damn, Kid," Lila said. "You're as full as a tick!"

"I ain't drunk," Merraux slurred, missing a step and nearly taking the two of them backwards down the stairwell. "I'm just celebratin', honey!"

"Well, why don't we celebrate in the room, if you'd be so kind?"

Merraux pulled the whore with him, barging into a room at the front of the hotel. The room was sparse and plain, dimly lit with a gas lamp. Just four wood-planked walls, a window next to a double bed and nightstand, along with a small table at the foot for a wash basin.

Merraux slung Lila from his arm roughly onto the bed, setting his bottle down on the night table. "Okay, whore," he sputtered drunkenly. "Get those duds off!"

"You just hold on, mister! I need to see some *dinero* before I do anything. Or you don't get nothin'." As Merraux started digging in his pockets, she added, "And if I were you, I'd think twice about bulldozing me. I've seen it all in my time, and don't need the lip of someone who's between hay and grass."

Through the alcoholic haze, Merraux had to admit she had a point. He'd hated being small in stature, with fair skin and a very boyish face. He tried to talk and act tougher than he really was, and knew the whiskey would run his mouth too much, just like it had in Laredo. But, he'd always had Fran to back him up, to pull his fat out of the fire.

Laredo. The Kid tried to put that miserable experience out of his mind. Will Dundee's assault of him had scared the piss and crap out of him. Literally.

As he watched Lila undo her bustle and strip off her wispy thin undergarments, exposing ripe, healthy breasts, the Kid was glad Fran wasn't here this time. Yeah, he was going to have a time of it tonight.

"Sorry, honey, it's the rotgut," Kid said regretfully.

"It usually is," the woman said, patting the bed beside her prone form.

Merraux grinned widely, stripping off his clothes in record time. He jumped into the bed with a whoop of joy, clad only in his boots, his gunbelt and his Stetson.

"What's all this?" Lila asked.

"I ain't doin' it any other way, darlin'!"

"If you say so, cowboy. Just don't mistake me for your horse with them spurs!"

As Kid Merraux and the prostitute rolled around in the bed, giggling uncontrollably among other things, he didn't hear the heavy footfalls coming up the hall outside his room.

The boot heels clacked loudly on the wood floor, but the Kid kept on attending to the lady beneath him. Only when there was a booming trio of knocks at the door, did Merraux halt his urgent, swift thrusts.

Another cannonade of raps sounded, buckling the door with each knock. "You got the wrong room, mister!" Kid shouted. "Beat it, or I'll bury you without a readin'!"

There was only silence for a response.

"Comon, now," Lila purred. "Before you lose it."

Just as Merraux proceeded to thrust his manhood into the woman beneath him once more, the door was kicked in with the force of a gunshot. The Kid yelped more from the sound than anything, but he rolled off the whore and looked toward the dimly lit doorway. A tall apparition stood there, and Merraux had to shake his head to realize that it was only a man.

A big bastard, that's for sure, but still just a man.

"What's the big idea, mister, breakin' down the door? You tryin' to horn in or somethin'?" Kid asked.

The black wraith stood there for a long moment. Then he took two slow steps forward. "What do you fear, Kid?" the man said in a voice that sounded like it came from the grave.

"Who...who are you, mister?"

The whore just sat there, trying to shield her body behind Merraux's. The tall, dark man paid her no attention, for his gaze was riveted solely on the Kid. Merraux squinted in the semi-darkness, trying to see the face of the man before him. It took him half a dozen heartbeats to finally make out who had barged into his hotel room.

"No," Merraux gasped. "What are you doin' here!"

The man wore a long, black greatcoat with a black, flat-brimmed hat. His face was like leather, his eyes cold, narrow and piercing. A long, handlebar mustache, waxed into points was plastered across his upper lip.

This was Will Dundee.

"'Give me chastity and continency...'," Dundee started.

With a screeching yell that shook the building, Kid Merraux leaped from the bed, hand grappling for the gun he wore on his hip.

He didn't realize until it was too late, the thong that held the sixgun in place was still hooked over the hammer of his weapon.

Will Dundee deftly drew his own sixgun and leveled it at the naked young man. He squeezed off three big .44 slugs that punched through Merraux's chest and sent him staggering back. He plowed into the window, shattering the glass, tumbling down onto the overhang of the hotel, and falling to the street below in a tangled heap.

"'...but not yet'!" Dundee chuckled.

Lila screamed like a banshee as the man in black calmly turned and walked out of the room.

Bel Jensen's first dose of reality was an agonizing chorus of children's screams. They bombarded his thoughts with such force, that when he opened his eyes, he expected angry kids to be surrounding him, attacking him, and ridiculing him. He waited for the moment when they would throw him to the ground, tear him apart and rip out his innards in a horrific display.

Bel now realized he stood in an alleyway next to the hotel. Covered in sweat, his heart raced and his ears rang. He looked up to the stars in the night sky, wondering what in blazes had just happened.

Feeling a sharp burning sensation in his hands, he yelped and brought them to his face. Expecting them to be blistered and mottled, he was surprised to see them unmarked.

Bel took a deep breath and leaned up against the side of the hotel for support. He noticed a group of townsfolk up ahead, their voices jabbering in confusion. He stood there, just wanting to get his strength back, using the building as a crutch, getting his nerves under control once again.

When Bel slowly crept up to the knot of people, he saw a naked body lying on its back, a pool of blood spreading beneath. Odd, Bel thought. The body was still wearing his boots and his gunbelt. A brown Stetson lay about ten feet away. Bel could imagine what the person had been doing prior to his demise.

He had been a young man, puny and baby-faced. Bel noticed the young kid had three bullets in the chest. That's strange, he thought, not remembering any gunfire.

"What's the matter?" Bel asked.

A grubby old-timer with a long beard spoke up. "A feller said that Will Dundee, the famous lawman, plumb went up and shot this boy. Right when he was in bed with a whore!"

Another man chimed in. "Ain't that somethin'! I heard that Dundee was over Californy way."

Bel knelt down and picked up the dead man's revolver, which lay only a few inches from his lifeless hand. A rivulet of blood slowly seeped into the initials "KM", etched into the wood near the butt of the weapon.

It dawned on him that this was one of the outlaws who'd taken part in the robbery in Dry Springs. "There was a bank robbery over in Dry Springs this morning," Bel informed them. "One of the robbers was a young man named Kid Merraux."

He held up the gun for the people to see, and they murmured in surprise. He dumped the bloody six-shooter on the dead man's chest and walked away from the onlookers.

Bel glanced around for his gray and saw it hitched across the street. How did he get there? Feeling apprehensive about his latest memory loss, along with the sounds and sensations that plagued him immediately thereafter, Bel was curious how long the blackout had lasted.

Where had he gone? What had he done?

He stood in the street for a few minutes, glancing around at the shoddy buildings, looking to the dark heavens, thinking things through in his mind.

He was stumped, and it bothered him to no end. Bel needed to unwind a bit from this latest event, contemplating a quick drink from the saloon. Then he would head back out on the trail to continue what had turned into a strange pursuit so far.

Bel ambled off down the street.

Chapter 10

Bel Jensen pushed through the batwing doors of the Silver Pan Saloon, his eyes burning immediately from the pall of cigar and cigarette smoke that hung in the air, his nose twitching from the sharp stench of stale sweat.

The saloon was nothing more than a shack put together in a hurry to cash in on the silver strike in the area, and to separate the money from the folks that came into camp.

The Silver Pan was a narrow, low-raftered room with a plain wooden bar. Opposite the bar, were a few small tables occupied by miners and hardcases playing cards. At the far end of the shack were a pot-bellied stove and a door that led out back.

Bel let his narrow eyes sweep the building, taking in each face, each man as they momentarily glanced at the new-comer, then went back to their business of drinking or poker.

Bel was not a drinking man. He'd have a beer once in a while, but he stayed away from the hard stuff, ever cognizant of the fact that it would be very easy for him to wallow in his misery and become a drunk. To have the whiskey drown out the harsh memories of his life was something that went through his mind now and again.

Plus, he'd tried rotgut once, and hated it. He'd once heard a man state that he never trusted anyone who didn't drink or play cards. Well, Bel thought, I guess I'll never be trustworthy in anyone's eyes, because he did neither.

Bel shuffled his way up to the wood-planked bar. A chubby, red-faced bartender with a walrus mustache was wiping his hands on a dirty apron, planting both large, hairy forearms on the bar. "Get yuh somethin', mister?"

"Sarsaparilla."

Behind him, Bel heard a few chuckles as he tossed a coin onto the bar, the barkeep nodding and getting his drink. He could detect a few mumblings, and Bel figured they were talking about him.

The bar man set the soft drink down in front of Bel, and he took the glass and raised it to his lips. That's when he heard the heavy rumbling noise seeming to be all around him.

Bel took a few sips, then put the glass down on the bar, glancing to his left ever so slowly, then to his right. The rumbling sounded like...a raging river or something. Bel wasn't sure.

Then a deep, booming voice intruded on the sounds Bel was hearing. "Hey, boy! What's that you got there?"

Bel turned to stare at a large, hairy man standing near the back door, a nasty sneer adorning his façade. The man was ugly and dirty, tobacco juice matted in his heavy beard. His clothes were soiled and sweaty, and he pushed his hat farther back on his head, his cold eyes focused on Bel, his grin widening, sticking a finger into his ear from some sort of discomfort.

"Yeah, you!" the man barked. "Men in here drink whiskey. Why don't you head on home to your mamma? She'll be needin' to wean yuh a little more on her tittie!"

There were a few guffaws from the seated onlookers and Bel's pulse quickened. He hated this man. There was something about him, something Bel couldn't quite nail down. Trying to keep his temper in check, Bel took another gulp of sarsaparilla, leaning his elbows back on the bar.

"I don't have a mother, mister," Bel said quietly. "You killed *yours*, didn't you? With an axe handle."

Bel took an indrawn breath. Where had that comment come from? That bit of information unsettled the onlookers, and Bel couldn't believe he'd spoken those words. The thought had just exploded into his consciousness like a cannon shell and before he knew what he was doing, he'd spoken.

The big, ugly man's eyes nearly popped out of their sockets. He was muttering curses under his breath. "That's a damn lie," he spat. "I never did no such thing to my momma! You'd best rein in that mouth of yours, boy! Before I decide to come over there and whip your little bottom blue!"

Bel heard the rushing water again. His eyes darted back and forth, wondering if the bar patrons heard it too. "You know what I think?" the hairy man said. "I think I saw you earlier in the hotel. What'd you do, boy? Go tattlin' to that cuss Will Dundee, so that he could shoot down Kid Merraux in cold blood? I don't cotton to that, boy! You're a damn coward!"

"And you're Dick James," Bel said. "Cold-blooded killer of a stationmaster and his wife, among others."

More mutterings came from the patrons as they cleared out of the way, leaving Bel facing the outlaw. "You son of a bitch!" James spat. "You better pull iron, boy!"

James had sidestepped closer to the rear door, his hand wavering over the gun on his hip. Bel came away from the bar, standing about ten feet away from the outlaw. "So help me God, I'll enjoy killing you, Dick James. You and Collier's bunch caused a lot of grief back in Dry Springs. Plus you tortured and killed that couple at the stage station. Somehow, some way, you're going to suffer! Like nothing you've ever experienced before!"

Bel hadn't been this angry in a long time. The man seemed to bring it out in him as he stared down this cold-hearted murderer. James emitted a guffaw before his hand flashed for his pistol. He was moving ever so quickly for a big man, and Bel crouched, his sixgun coming out of the holster, leveling on Dick James.

Bel's gun flamed first, bullets punching holes in the wall of a protruding partition opposite the back door. James had dived behind the partition, then thrust his gun forward, snapping off a few sizzling rounds that splintered the bar near Bel's head, spraying him with bits of wood. The bar folks froze in their tracks as Bel leaped to his feet and saw James ducking out the door.

He heard the pattering hooves of a horse, knowing James was going to make a run for it. Bel dashed out the back door with his gun tracking, but there was no horse and rider.

He retraced his steps back into the saloon, crashing through the batwings, coming to stand out front in the dusty street.

That was when Bel saw the horse and its rider, Dick James, come galloping from the alley. Bel tried to raise his gun but James plowed his mount forward, the horse's shoulder clipping Bel, knocking him the ground, tumbling head over heels.

The last thing Bel saw was the dust kicked up by the retreating rider. He felt blood trickling down his face, as he descended into darkness, the sound of a rushing torrent of water slowly fading.

Bel Jensen came to, feeling like his head was crushing under a steel press. He saw one of the townsfolk shaking him, while others gathered around.

"Hey, feller, you okay?"

It took Bel a few moments to focus his vision as he tried to sit up. The man helping him was the same old-timer with the beard who he'd seen soon after Kid Merraux died. "Take it easy, son," the man urged. "You had a nasty spill."

"Where's my gun? I need my gun."

The old codger placed the sixgun in Bel's hand as he staggered unsteadily to his feet. "How long was I out?" Bel asked.

"Oh, not more than a few minutes. The boys and I came rushin' out not long after you."

"I...I have to find that man," Bel said.

"You want help, feller?"

"No! I'll do this alone."

His head pounding unmercifully, Bel made his way to his horse, holstering his gun as he mounted the gray, putting spurs to his flanks, racing out of Hollins.

The trail out of town was good for the first couple of miles, then got progressively rougher and rockier. Bel wasn't really following sign, but like this morning when Dry Springs drew him in, he was going on gut feeling and instinct.

Bel left the trail altogether, his horse trotting along at an easy gait. The moon cast a multitude of shadows across the desert terrain, its radiance full and bright in the night sky.

Bel's head hurt like the blazes, and he began mumbling to his horse to try to put the pain out of his mind. "It'll be fine. Everything will be fine."

Bel tried to understand the events back in Hollins. With an urgent sense of dread, Bel realized that it had happened again.

Just like with the bully cowhand. He lost track of time and place.

Bel didn't feel right. He felt stranger than he ever had before.

He reached up to feel the clotted blood matted in his hair. His temples throbbed, and he knew something else was happening to him. Bel didn't know if he could stop it.

Bel shut his eyes, immersed in the swirling, dark mist that was forming all around him. After a moment, the cloud peeled away, and he saw a hairy, giant of a man sitting near a small campfire.

Dick James. It had to be.

His horse dipped into a rocky arroyo lined with mesquite, the clacking of the hooves on stone bringing Bel out of his reverie.

He urged his gray up the stony embankment, reining him in abruptly. Bel scanned the area ahead and saw the dim outline of low, rugged hills. In the sky, he could almost detect a yellowish glow.

A campfire possibly?

The murky blackness embraced him.

* * *

The Figure peered around a large rock and into a small clearing, seeing Dick James sitting down to some grub, beans cooking over the fire. He sensed an eagerness emanating in the man. As if he wanted to get to his destination. The Figure clawed His way into the outlaw's thoughts. He could tell the man detested women.

Had beaten them.

Mutilated them.

Killed them.

This one deserved to die, The Figure thought. He smiled as He watched the outlaw eat his meal. Then The Figure saw Dick James wincing, sticking his finger into one ear from obvious pain.

The Figure began to hear a deep rumbling in his head. There was a torrent of rushing water, and He became swept up in its cool, relaxing embrace. Then the cries of a child interrupted the reverie. A child calling for his father.

The Figure snapped back to reality as He saw the outlaw still picking at his ear. Even with the moon out, The Figure stood bathed in shadows.

Dick James sensed something. He scooped up his rifle and brought the weapon to his shoulder.

"What do you fear, Dick?" The Figure's voice was slow, seductive, and totally lethal.

"Who the hell are you?"

"No one in particular."

"Whaddaya want?"

"You!"

The Figure took a step forward, chuckling as he felt the ripples of terror running through His victim's body.

"You better set up camp some place else, mister," James' voice quivered.

"Are you afraid, Dick?"

"No, I'm not!"

The Figure reveled in the man's anxiety, sneering at His hapless prey. *"You should be!"*

The rifle in Dick's hands trembled. "Damn it, how do you know me?"

"I know what's inside you. I know all about your childhood."

"What?"

"That day on the lake. Long ago, with your father."

Dick James whimpered and sweat poured from his face. His breath came in ragged gasps.

"I know what happened." The Figure took a step forward.

"No! Stop it!"

"'I must be cruel only to be kind', Dick!"

The torrent of water raged and the outlaw's eyes bulged out in ungodly terror. He unleashed a deep, piercing cry that echoed through the hills. No one heard him.

Chapter 11

Bel had lost Dick James.

Or had he?

He remembered seeing the glow in the night sky, what he thought was a campfire. Then...nothing. Now, he was still in the rocky, rugged terrain, surrounded by patches of grass, some ocotillo bushes and prickly-pear.

Bel had found himself trotting his horse through the Dos Cabezos, not knowing how long he'd been out of touch with reality. He realized it was still dark, probably close to midnight, figuring it would be a good idea to settle down for the night. He'd try to pick up Dick James' trail in the morning.

Bel found a clearing in which to set up camp. He tied his gray to a bush, then began laying out his bedroll. Finally, he decided to start a fire to keep warm through the chilly night in the high, desert mountain terrain.

Fifteen minutes later, with a small fire burning, Bel was stretched out under the stars, head resting on his saddle, trying to let sleep overtake him. It wasn't easy. He was exhausted after the late-night action in Hollins, and prayed for a night's sleep without any nightmares or pain-wracked images.

Bel, curled up on his side with blankets up to his chin, heard something behind him. His gunbelt was next to his head and his hand reached out, feeling for the reassuring wood grips of his .45 Colt. Had Dick James followed him, looking to dry-gulch him in his sleep?

Bel once again heard the sound of someone moving in the brush. His hand was gripping his sixgun. Taking a deep breath, he yanked the gun from the holster, threw off the blankets and whirled around to confront his adversary.

About ten feet away, where his horse was tethered, was a large rock. The campfire didn't provide much light, but Bel saw a dark figure sitting there watching him. He leveled his gun and thumbed back the hammer.

"Who are you and what do you want?" Bel demanded.

"Put the gun away, *gringo,* I won't hurt you."

Bel squinted through the semi-darkness, and could see the man was wearing dark clothes, and a Roman collar. He was a lanky, middle-aged Hispanic man with thin, graying hair, his back propped up against the rock. He looked familiar but...

"Do you not recognize me, Belial?" the priest asked.

"I don't..." Bel was quite shocked to say the least to have this man calling him by his given name. He studied the man for a few long moments more, then it finally came it him, and Bel lowered his gun.

"Father Garcia!"

"Yes, it is I, Belial."

"But, what...how did you get all the way out here?"

"I had to find you after all these years."

"But, why?"

"To tell you. To make you understand. *Comprende?*"

"Tell me what?"

Father Garcia got up to his knees, leaning forward, his face shadowed by the firelight. Bel could detect a few large, angry red patches on the priest's face, almost resembling open sores or boils.

"You don't remember, *gringo*?"

"What are you talking about, Father?" Bel was sort of confused. Why had Father Garcia left the mission, traveled across two states to try to find him and then when he had found him, start in with this cryptic nonsense?

Father Garcia moved in a step closer. To Bel's horror, the priest's horribly blackened face greeted him, his hair all but singed off.

"You should know," Garcia growled. "It was all your fault!"

"What was my fault?"

Bel couldn't believe this was playing out before him. It wasn't real, he was telling himself. It just couldn't be real.

Then Father Garcia appeared only inches away from Bel, and Bel wanted to wretch. One of Garcia's eyeballs was melted away, leaving only a dark, ruined socket. His entire face was as black as pitch, with clumps of skin oozing off, revealing ivory bone. The odor that emanated from the Garcia figure was too much for Bel to bear. It was the unmistakable smell of scorched flesh.

"They've come for you, too!" Garcia taunted.

Bel Jensen turned away from the horrid, pulped figure and saw the short, child-like phantoms walking slowly toward him from the other direction.

"Here we are, Belial!" they sang.

There were almost a dozen or so of the small creatures lurching unsteadily, with their arms out, the whites of their eyes bright in the darkness. Their bodies were also decomposing, black and pulpy, with bones protruding through the ghastly masses.

"STAY AWAY FROM ME! ALL OF YOU!"

"Why did you do it, Belial?" the child-wraiths screeched.

"No, no, no!"

Bel, on his haunches, began to scramble away from the oncoming ghouls. He didn't see the Father Garcia-thing as Bel backed up to the large rock. The children closed in on him, their bony, mottled arms outstretched, coming for him. Then he saw the terrible Garcia figure at his side, his peeled back lips near Bel's ear.

"Why did you do it, Belial?" he croaked hoarsely.

"I DON'T KNOW WHAT I'VE DONE, FOR CHRIST'S SAKE!" Bel screamed. "Leave me alone!"

The Father Garcia-thing stood up and joined the child phantoms, hovering over Bel's stretched out form. Bel's heart was hammering, sweat pouring from his body as the group reached out with their skeletal hands as one, fingers curled menacingly.

"We're waiting, Belial!" they chanted.

With a blood-curdling scream, Bel held up his arms to ward off the attacking monsters...then noticed that he was all alone in the desert night.

Bel Jensen, frightened beyond belief, passed out.

* * *

In the early morning, Sheriff Thompson and his four-man posse spotted the buzzards circling in the distance. Many of the townspeople hadn't been willing to go after the likes of the Collier gang, hence the lack of volunteers. That was okay with Thompson. He didn't need any greenhorns with itchy trigger-fingers traipsing along fouling things up.

The posse had galloped out of Hollins earlier this morning after hearing about the demise of Kid Merraux. The townsfolk told them about the appearance of a young cowpoke right after the shooting, along with the subsequent ruckus in the Silver Pan Saloon involving Dick James.

The sheriff guessed who they meant. The strange youngster from Dry Springs.

The group of riders came over the rise of the hills, spotting the corpse amid clumps of mesquite. Thompson signaled his men to a halt, drawing up rein about twenty yards from the body.

"Judas Priest!" the lawman muttered, nervously stuffing a wad of tobacco into his mouth.

It looked as if the buzzards had just started their feast. The sheriff drew his gun and fired into the air, discouraging the scavengers from further nourishment.

Thompson and the men with him glanced nervously at each other, then down the trail at the corpse, wanting to draw it out as long as possible, not having to investigate the dead man.

Thompson nodded at the closest rider, a clean-shaven man who wore a vest, chaps and rawhide gloves, motioning toward the body. The sheriff knew he was a ranch hand who never backed away from a fight.

"Let's go, Wylie," Thompson said, then addressing the other men. "The rest of you boys stay put."

Reluctantly, Wylie and Thompson slowly made their way to the corpse. Wylie stifled a gasp as he stared down into the horrid mess. "Damnation! His face is gone!"

Thompson grunted his agreement, his jaw moving methodically. "Bad way to go."

The eyes had been plucked out, leaving only mushy, bloody sockets. The cheeks, pock-marked in a dozen places, revealed grisly blossoms of crimson. The mouth was agape in a halted scream. The lawman nudged the body with the toe of his boot and saw something peculiar, his eyes straining to focus. "What the hell is that?"

Curious now, Thompson pushed the corpse onto its stomach. Both men saw the water leaking from the body's mouth, pooling in the dirt.

Wylie finally broke the eerie silence. "We're in the middle of a desert and this poor bastard's full of water?"

"Yeah," the lawman agreed. "Like he drowned."

"This is ungodly!" Wylie said quietly.

"Then we should probably do the most Christian thing," Thompson said. "We ought to bury the gent."

As much as the sight sickened him, Thompson believed the corpse should be tended to. Every man, he figured, should have the proper burial.

After the task was completed, both men walked back to their mounts, slid into the saddle, and left the gory scene behind them.

If that was a member of the Collier gang, things were definitely amiss. Thompson could have sworn that it was Dick James. He knew from the wanted bills that James was a despicable excuse for a human being.

Well, the sheriff thought, the man didn't look so mean now, did he?

Then his thoughts roamed to that drifter from Dry Springs. He obviously had confronted James back in Hollins. Had he cornered him here and killed him? Somehow, Thompson didn't think the kid was that cold, killing a man, and leaving him for the buzzards. But then again, after looking into the drifter's eyes, maybe he did have a stone-cold heart.

Something had been bugging Thompson on the trail, but it just now dawned on him what it was. That stranger...he sort of looked familiar, the sheriff thought. He was pretty sure he'd never met the youngster. I'd remember meeting one like that. Unless...

The sheriff tried to focus on the trail ahead. He knew this area somewhat, and figured there was a patch of terrain that would be perfect for what he had in mind.

Putting Dick James and the drifter out of his mind, Sheriff Zeke Thompson mentally prepared himself for executing his plan.

The lawman smiled.

Chapter 12

Bel Jensen was losing control.

He stood on a bluff overlooking a dilapidated, two-story ranch house, a barn and some small outbuildings situated in what had once been a lush, green valley. He'd ridden out of the mountains the next morning, which had spilled into this sprawling sea of low hills and grass.

He'd started all this yesterday, thinking that the inexplicable pull toward Dry Springs would be the right thing to do.

But now, after witnessing the bank robbery, and meeting the Desmond girl, guessing that tracking down the robbers was what he had to do? Bel wasn't so sure.

He'd been in his own personal hell since this all began. The blackouts in the last day had rattled him, frightening him to his very core.

Sure, over the years he'd often wondered what he was, where he came from. Why he wasn't like other people. Sometimes, Bel would wonder if he *really* was a demon. If there really was a Satan, did He send him from the underworld, into this world to wreak havoc upon these...mortals??

Why? For what purpose?

Bel would reason if that were the case, then he'd failed long ago. Bel knew deep inside he was not an evil man. He was an honest and good person saddled with some sort of power he couldn't understand. And, he was never sure of what that power was, considering he was never conscious whenever it had its hold on him.

Plus, if he were Satan's minion, and had not done what his Master had ordained, wouldn't this all powerful creature of evil have him vanquished already? Although, Bel knew that Satan had a passion for suffering. Was this Bel's lot in life? To suffer?

Bel had once heard a man speak who was ridiculed for thinking there was life elsewhere beyond planet Earth. And that aliens had come here long, long ago and planted the seeds of life on the world in which they now lived. At times, Bel would look at himself in the mirror and wonder, was he one of those "aliens"? Was he born on another world, far away from this one? Was that the reason he couldn't remember anything before his arrival at the mission?

Was he here on some sort of assignment? Maybe he'd lost contact with the other members of his race. Or maybe these aliens were manipulating him? Maybe they were planning on taking over this planet, and were using him and his power for their own purposes?

Or had his parents been witches, like he'd read about in books, some place called Salem. Had they abandoned him at the mission all those years ago? If so, why?

Bel had chewed on all these explanations for his being different over the years. They didn't seem right, but how would he know for sure?

He didn't know why he'd come here, to this bluff on the edge of the valley. Last night still ran chills through his body. Bel tried to concentrate on where he had been prior to his confrontation with those...those...creatures.

He drew a blank.

It haunted him for what remained of the night, depriving him of sleep. Pain-wracked images swept through his mind the whole time-- screams of agony, nameless faces crying out his name, and that intense smell of something burning.

As Bel continued to take in the old, weathered ranch building below, he thought that going down there might somehow shed light on his recent memory lapses.

Bel didn't understand why, but two words seemed to flash into his thoughts. "The...Figure."

He got back to his horse, slipped into the saddle and set out to discover what lay ahead.

Something raced through Bel's mind.

Something mammoth. Atrocious. Hideous.

Bel Jensen's vision became obscured.

* * *

Rance Welby hated waiting. But that was all he could do at the moment. Until Dick and the Kid showed up, he was stuck. What was taking them so long?

The ranch house hadn't been used in over ten years. "The Man" had "evicted" the owners, God rest their souls. Since then, Welby and the gang had used it as a hideout on more than one occasion.

With a deep foreboding dread, Welby kept thinking that they should have passed on the Dry Springs bank job. He also couldn't shake the notion that someday the Devil himself would rise up from Hell and drag him down into his fiery realm if he kept on this outlaw path.

I have to calm down, he thought. From a rickety swing on the back porch, Welby made his way inside toward the front of the weathered ranch building, where a study still filled with dust-covered volumes of books stood. He figured on relaxing and reading some verses from the Bible.

Welby passed Francis Collier on his left, who was making himself some grub in the kitchen, nodding to his cousin as he walked by. The well-dressed outlaw entered the hallway leading to the study.

Down the corridor, but connected to the kitchen was the dining area, where a rotted table stood, with rickety wooden chairs falling apart, some missing legs, others tipped over. Opposite the dining room was the parlor where a thick layer of dust covered the settee, the Hitchcock chair and a few pieces of Belter furniture.

He spotted the young, rough-featured man with a Colt revolver scrambling inside the front door, angling to take cover directly by the side door frame of the study. Welby barely pulled his gun when the intruder's weapon roared in the close confines of the hall. He felt a stab of pain as one of the slugs grazed his side.

Welby staggered toward the opposite end of the corridor, noticing the young man had entered the study through the side door, peering around the open double doors that led to the dining room. Welby snapped off a few rounds that splintered the wood near the doorjamb.

What in God's name was going on? Welby thought. Was this a man from the posse? How'd they find this place so fast? He didn't have time to contemplate the answer as the intruder's six-gun boomed again. Welby was moving quickly, barreling into a closet at the other end of the hall opposite the kitchen, the hot lead buzzing by his ear.

"Who are you? What do you want?" Welby yelled.

A brief stillness settled in as he waited for an answer, the walls seeming to close in on him in the cramped atmosphere. He heard shuffling in the kitchen and figured Collier was getting out of there.

"What do you fear, Rance?"

The voice had Welby petrified. It sounded malicious, like pure poison. "You're dead!" Welby shouted, his lower lip quivering.

"I know what you fear!"

Welby couldn't stop shaking. He grabbed the crucifix he wore around his neck and bowed his head, tears beginning to stream from his eyes.

"'Oh, my God, I am heartily sorry for having offended Thee,'" he whimpered, "'and I detest all my sins because of Thy just punishments, but most of all because they have offended Thee, my God, who art all good and deserving of all my love...'"

Welby didn't bother finishing his Act of Contrition, stumbling as he burst into the middle of the hall, leveling his revolver.

He stopped dead in his tracks.

Standing dead ahead of Welby was a large form. It looked human somewhat, but when Welby scrutinized it more closely, he saw that it wasn't.

Its torso had a desiccated, reddish tint. The head, grotesque and scraggy, sported a thin mustache and goatee. The red glowing eyes were cruel and hard, with a pair of horns protruding from the beast's upper forehead. Two cloven hooves and a forked tail swishing impatiently back and forth completed the Hellish form.

The devil had finally come a calling.

"'Lasciate ogni speranza voi ch'entrate'!" the beast hissed.

Abandon all hope, you who enter.

"No!" Welby cried. "It can't be!"

With a horrified shriek, the outlaw brought up his weapon, but the beast already had his six-gun aimed. A bullet struck Rance Welby through the cheek, exiting in a sticky spray, the body tumbling lifeless to the floor.

* * *

The Figure calmly stalked his last victim. He sensed confusion in the outlaw leader. Then the entity began to receive strong vibrations from the man He closed in on. It was a certain fright the outlaw experienced as a child.

A dream.

No, a nightmare.

The Figure grinned maliciously. A hideous monstrosity filtered into His thoughts. Now He could kill the helpless criminal!

The Figure burst out into the main ranch yard as Collier stood near the pole corral cursing at his unsaddled horse. Spotting movement in his peripheral vision, the outlaw spun to face The Figure behind him.

The entity saw His adversary's gun flame, just as He fired his. Collier's slug burned a furrow across the top of His shoulder. The entity growled at the burning sensation, not relishing the sensation of pain.

It just made him angrier. This weakling would have to pay the price dearly!

Then He noticed that His shot had plowed into Collier's stomach. The man gasped in pain, his gun falling from numb fingers. He staggered back a few paces, seeing The Figure before him. The bank robber noticed the emptiness in His gaze.

"I give up." Collier struggled to stay on his feet. "I'm all done in."

"You left that woman without a father," The Figure replied coldly.

"Wait a minute! If you're not with the posse, then..."

"I CAN BE WHATEVER YOU FEAR!"

Collier's knees began to buckle as he shook his head in disbelief. The entity's eyebrows cocked. *"What about your nightmares?"*

Collier's face went white and sick. His breath came in large gasps, and his body convulsed in fright. "I—I don't know what you're talking about," Collier sputtered.

"Yes, you do," The Figure hissed. *"I know what terrorizes you--I know your dreams."*

Collier wept now. "No, go away!"

"Did it look something like this?"

Collier's eyes, wide with terror, watched The Figure before him turn into a ghastly, quivering blob of contorting limbs and flesh. In a matter of seconds, the entity formed a solid, living thing.

Francis Collier screamed in high pitch.

The familiar object of his nightmares was enormous, over seven feet tall. Its bulbous midsection was like a cockroach's, rust-colored and repulsive. It had muscular hind legs, the toes clawed. The head resembled a dragon, having a scabrous snout that bared razor sharp teeth. The blood-red eyes seethed with fury. Two slimy tentacles jutted from the shoulders, slithering about, seeking its prey.

Collier continued to scream, frozen in utter shock, as one of the tentacles lashed out and gripped him around the neck. There was a soft, squishy sound, with Francis Collier becoming decapitated, blood jetting out like a geyser in all directions. The other tentacle ensnared the headless body and flung it away like a rag doll, the corpse smashing through the corral poles, leaving a trail of crimson in its wake.

Chapter 13

Sheriff Zeke Thompson approached the ranch house alone. He grinned widely as he thought back to the trail. He told the four other men to go on over the next ridge, that he needed to check on his horse's shoe, getting them to think his mount was favoring one leg.

Thompson was afraid that it wasn't going to work, but the men relented and galloped on, while he waited for them to ride out of sight. Then he trotted his horse up the mountain a ways, until he could find an ideal spot where he could see the group.

After that, he hunkered down with his Winchester and began to pick off the posse members one by one. He shot them from their saddles, with only Wylie getting off a few rounds toward his position. But, they never even hit close to the sheriff.

Yeah, Wylie was game all right, Thompson thought. He was a good kid. Too bad it had to end this way.

Now he would meet up with Collier, and they would split the money. Of course, they'd always planned to eliminate the other gang members, but recent events had taken care of it already.

Thompson saw a lone figure standing in the corral, and his lawman's senses went on alert. He urged his horse faster, as he thought he recognized the person.

Aw, hell! It was that damn kid from Dry Springs! Thompson was afraid of that. That meddling drifter had decided to try to be a hero and go after the Collier gang all by himself!

The sheriff unhooked the thong that held his revolver in place, pulling it from the holster to allow easy access. As he got closer, Thompson saw a large, dark stain in the dirt, along with a rounded object lying nearby. Christ Almighty! It...it looked like a human head!

He felt his stomach churning, and in one brief moment, realized he might not leave this place alive.

* * *

Bel Jensen, bathed in sweat, darted his eyes back and forth as he saw the rider approaching. When he spotted the decapitated head lying amid the pool of blood directly in front of where he stood, he gasped in terror.

He knew it was Francis Collier's head. The bulging eyes wide with fright, mouth open aghast in a halted scream, and tongue hanging out from blood-spattered lips.

Bel Jensen felt the blood pounding at his ears, his entire head throbbing from the horrific sight. Had he done this? How could he have ripped the outlaw's head off? There was nothing about that was sharp, and all's he had was his gun...and bare hands.

Flickering images swept through Bel's mind. They were indistinct at first, just bits and pieces of experiences from his life—a crack of thunder, his first memory standing outside the door of the mission, his day-to-day life through the years at the mission with the other orphans.

As Bel stood there watching the rider come ever closer, the images in his mind began to sharpen, and he couldn't explain why, but with this latest blackout, things and events began to fall into place once and for all. The revelation hit him like a hammer blow.

He now understood who he was and what he was.

But, before he could dwell on that further, his mind was processing that last fateful night at the mission.

A forgotten memory was breaking through.

Right after Micah MacLean's death, and a younger Bel Jensen wandered back to the mission in that torrential downpour...

Bel was completely drenched as he staggered up the hill to the mission, the rain still coming down in thick sheets. The storm camouflaged the fact that tears were still streaming down his cheeks and Bel was uttering painful sobs from witnessing the death of his friend.

Bel made it to the front porch of the two-story Victorian house, bent over with exhaustion. He tried to take in deep breaths to calm himself down, but the sobs kept wracking his body as he reached for the doorknob.

Locked.

"Damn it! God...DAMN IT!" he bellowed, punching the heavy door with his fist.

With all his might, Bel launched his boot out and connected with the door, flinging it open. He stood in the foyer, breaths coming in pitiful wheezes. To his left was the front room, while directly ahead was the hallway leading to the kitchen. Parallel to the hallway was the staircase that led up to the second floor.

Bel saw a figure making its way down, holding a coal lamp to see what the disturbance was about.

It was Sister Mary. Bel cursed inwardly. Why did it have to be her?

"What are you doing, Belial?" she cracked harshly. "Busting down the door like a thief? You'll wake the other children!"

"Sister Mary," Bel said, trying to keep his voice from cracking. "I'm sorry I made such a fuss. The door was locked, and it's pouring down rain and..."

"I don't want to hear your excuses, you DEMON!" Sister Mary hissed. "You have no business in town this late at night, carousing with the marshal, doing God-knows-what!" She jerked her head, motioning back up the stairs. "Now get upstairs and get in bed. Tomorrow we'll have a long talk about your future here at the mission!"

Her words stung. He wished so badly that Sister Katherine was still here, so he could talk to her about how he was feeling and to have some comfort from her. But, no, there was only this old crone who hid behind the habit of God. The pain hurt so much his chest ached with frustration.

"Don't you even have a clue what happened tonight, Sister Mary? Don't you even care?"

"I'll hear nothing from you! Get out of my sight, Belial!"

"The marshal was killed tonight, you old hag!" Bel said with gritted teeth. "Some drunk put a forty-five slug into his stomach, and I couldn't do anything about it! Damn you for your lack of compassion!"

Her eyes blazed with fury as she thrust out the coal lamp threateningly at Bel. "You! You probably got him killed! You are nothing but a BEAST! You hear? You are the spawn of Satan, you pathetic...BASTARD! And by tomorrow you will be gone from this holy sanctuary. Finally we will be rid of your scourge! Do you understand that, BELIAL?"

The sobs stopped suddenly and Bel felt all the pain, all the frustrations, every ounce of internal strife melt away from his body. It was like he had become at peace with all his surroundings.

But his gaze hardened, and he saw Sister Mary noticing his eyes darkening to black coals. She stepped back, her mouth opening in fright.

"I understand," Bel said in a deep rattling voice that was not his own, "that you have always feared something besides God." He smiled at Sister Mary, a cold, detached grin. "And now you'll meet that fear...*in the flesh!*"

"What do you mean?" Sister Mary said, a bit of trepidation in her voice. "Let's just go upstairs, Belial."

Bel's head cocked curiously, the mischievous grin widening on his façade. "Do you like bees, Sister Mary?" the young man asked in a playful, yet deadly tone.

Before the nun's eyes, Bel's body was transformed into a gelatinous blob, sprouting long insectile wings and manifesting hairy appendages. The huge flying beast filled the entire foyer and more as it hovered over the terrified nun.

Sister Mary could only utter a hoarse rattle as she retreated back toward the stairway, but tripped on the bottom step. The coal lamp fell from her grasp as she sprawled out on the stairs, the hot oil splashing all over the floor and her body.

It quickly ignited into hot flame, and Bel came out of his trance just in time to see the flailing, screeching figure of Sister Mary consumed by fire. More flames marched up the walls and the stairs as Bel's look of horror overtook him.

He held up his arms as if to ward off the wall of fire that was growing, back-peddling to the front door, turning sharply, stumbling onto the front porch.

Bel ended up crawling down the front steps and into the yard as he could begin to hear stirrings upstairs from the house. Harsh crackling and popping assaulted his ears as Bel, completely paralyzed with fear, wheezing like some animal, sat there in the cool wet grass and watched the main house go up in flames.

He began to hear terrible screams and calls for help, but the young man could do nothing but lay there and watch the spectacle before him. He thought he saw someone break an upstairs window. Could that be Sister Lupe? Or was that Father Garcia?

Then the figure collapsed out of sight, with more screams, this time of children that would be etched in Bel's subconscious forever. Flames burst from the front windows, sparing no part of the house, as it became a searing sea of doom.

When Bel finally did start to understand what was happening, he shakily got to his feet and staggered off toward the barn nearby. With the townsfolk probably side-tracked by the killing of their marshal, it would take them a few minutes to get people up the hill to see what was happening at the mission.

But, it wouldn't take long. The flames would bring them like moths. Bel didn't want to be around and take the blame for this horrible disaster.

The rain had been reduced to a light drizzle as he got to the barn and re-saddled his gray, mounted the horse and galloped out. He pulled up in front of the burning house, not hearing any signs of life, save for the sounds of a crackling fire.

Bel Jensen gave it one last, long look, then turned solemnly and rode off into the night...

Bel could almost remember the intense heat of the flames, the ungodly screams of the children as they were trapped in their beds, waiting for the inevitable moment when they would burn to death. The realization began to take hold of Bel, and the tears started to come.

"My god! What have I done?"

Sobs wracked Bel's body as the rider was still about a hundred yards off. Knowing that he'd abandoned all those holy people and children to die, it made him feel completely and utterly worthless.

But, then like the flame that had engulfed Sister Mary, another one was lit in the pit of Bel's stomach. Somehow he knew the man walking his horse toward him now was the mastermind, the brains behind the Collier gang robbing the Dry Springs bank. Rage was now enveloping the young man.

He hoped that The Figure would take over and deal a slow, punishing death to the rider before him. Bel wasn't able to explain, however, the words that formed in his mouth.

"I can be whatever you fear," he whispered, being somewhat calmed by his own words, but still being inwardly enraged.

Zeke Thompson swung down from his horse, his hand resting near the butt of his weapon.

SNAKE! MAKE HIM SUFFER!

The image once again hit Bel Jensen, of a huge coiled serpent ready to strike. Except this time, no black void enveloped him.

"Howdy, sheriff," Bel greeted, wiping tears from his eyes. "Fancy meeting you here."

Thompson cracked a crooked grin. "You ballin' there, boy? That ain't so manly now, is it?" He waved his hand. "Don't matter, because you're in a pack of trouble, mister!"

"Why is that?"

"Bein' a sheriff is a risky job. I need somethin' to look forward to." Thompson's face turned ugly with rage, and tobacco juice dribbled from his mouth. "You meddled in business that don't concern you!

The gang got ten thou' from that job, boy! The owners wouldn't have been able to hold out after a loss like that. Me and Francis were gonna buy them out and be rich men!"

Bel's eyes pierced the lawman's. They were like hot daggers that ripped into the man's soul. "You'd better light out of here, sheriff," he said in a graveyard tone. "Or you just might get a sting from a serpent out of your past."

"Huh?"

"You know what I mean."

A nerve-jangling hiss seemed to emanate from Bel Jensen. Thompson started, as if touched by a spark. He looked about at his feet, expecting to see a coiled rattler. His head shot up to meet Bel's teasing stare, grunting with embarrassment. He flushed, smiling acceptingly as if a joke had been told on him.

The crooked lawman backed up a few paces, flexing the fingers on his right hand as Bel took a step back, dropping his hand near his side.

"You want me to notify any kin when I kill you, boy?" Thompson asked.

"Don't have any."

"Guess that's it then," Thompson said.

"'Let justice be done'."

Thompson spoke low, but Bel could make out the words clearly. "'Now is the end come upon thee, and I will send mine anger upon thee'."

Bel's pulse quickened as he remembered back in time, to that fateful rainy night when Micah MacLean had met his fate, and the mystery man who'd done the deed.

"You!" Bel accused, speaking in a whisper of death. "I remember you! You killed a friend of mine years ago in Sanctuary!"

The words seemed to hit Thompson like a blow, and he finally recognized Bel's face from time gone by. He'd been nothing but a loafer back then, always in a drunken stupor and seemingly at trail's end.

Thompson's eyes widened at the revelation, and his hand, quick as lightning went for the gun on his hip. Bel, seeing the move, went for his own six-shooter, confident that this was the fastest draw he'd ever made.

But, as Bel watched the showdown in a sort of mind-bending slow-motion, he saw Thompson's gun come up level a hair quicker than his.

Thompson's gun muzzle was exploding in hot white flame, and Bel felt a blazing sting crash into him while his own gun roared.

Through the blue-white haze of powder smoke, Bel saw Thompson staggering, blood pouring from the side of his head. Bel noticed that his left arm and shoulder was numb, and he looked down to see the shirt ripped at the elbow. Bel had been lucky, the bullet having scraped along the side of his arm. He could feel the faintest trickle of blood underneath his shirt.

Bel saw Thompson fall onto his bottom, disoriented, but still trying to aim his gun for another shot. Bel sighted down his Colt and triggered a .45 round that drilled Thompson's gun hand, sending the weapon flying and tumbling the lawman onto his back.

Bel walked forward with his sixgun aimed, not trusting Thompson for not having a hideout pistol of some kind. He came to stand over the cowering man, tobacco juice bubbling from his mouth, running down the sides of his face.

The lawman emitted gasping sobs of both pain and alarm, his hand clutching at what was left of his left ear, as blood seeped copiously from between his fingers.

"I...I remember you now," Thompson gasped. "I didn't know what I was doin' back then. Guess you could say I wasn't on the wagon."

Bel thumbed back the hammer on his gun and Thompson spasmed with the harsh sound. "Just get it over with, son," Thompson urged him.

"Now you listen to me," Bel rasped, "I'm not gonna kill you because there's been enough killing already. No, I'm gonna do worse. I'm gonna spread the word that Zeke Thompson is a thief, a drunk and a killer of innocent people. I'll tell it to anyone who will listen to me, and *they will listen to me!*"

Bel kneeled down over the prone form of Thompson, could see the lawman was horrified at his words. He tried to back away from Bel, but Bel was right there in his face. "You won't be able to go anywhere without people knowing your name and face and hounding you to the ends of the earth for the deeds you've committed!

"So you get on your horse and get out of here, or so help me, I'll give you a sting you won't soon forget. If I hear that Zeke Thompson is around these parts, you'd better have eyes in the back of your head, because you won't even see me coming! You hear me, mister?"

Bel watched a stain spread across the front of the lawman's pants, smelling something rank and putrid. He stood up and backed away a few steps. "I reckon you do."

In a flash, Thompson was up and staggering back to his mount, galloping off in a cloud of dust. Bel watched him go and shouted after him, "TO THE ENDS OF THE EARTH, ZEKE THOMPSON!"

Thompson's horse galloped faster.

Bel thought for a moment, remembering the sheriff's words to him before the lead started to fly. "I'll be damned," Bel said. "'Now is the end come upon thee, and I will send mine anger upon thee, and will judge thee according to thy ways, and will recompense upon thee all thine abominations'."

The Holy Bible. *Ezekiel*, chapter seven, verse three.

Bel Jensen felt drained, as if an incredible weight had been lifted from his chest. He collapsed to his knees, getting all knotted up on the inside. It had been a long, dusty journey.

Bel Jensen smiled. For the first time in years, he smiled a grand smile, feeling the tears welling up in his eyes once again. For he had finally triumphed against the power he never knew he had. Maybe he could live a normal life from now on.

He felt the agonizing pull of loneliness setting in. His mind filled with thoughts of that young woman whose path he'd crossed. The softness of her skin. Those beautiful eyes. That inner strength he had felt. He knew what he had to do as he headed for his horse.

He would return to Dry Springs. And make one final journey into his past.

Then maybe he could settle down at last. But, Bel Jensen did know one thing, even though it wouldn't bring her loved one back.

Ella Desmond could rest easy now.

Chapter 14

The Revelation

Two days later, under an overcast sky of gun-metal gray, Bel Jensen ambled his steed over the rise and saw the town of Dry Springs loom in the distance. Hanging from his saddle bags were the sacks of money stolen by the Collier gang.

As Bel turned his horse onto the dusty, main street, he saw a large group of people gathered near the end of town. Bel noticed that they all wore black, and he figured it was for the funeral of Ella Desmond's father.

Bel brought his mount to a halt in the center of town outside the bank as the townsfolk came closer. It was only three days ago that violence had invaded this sleepy little hamlet, with lead flying, and the town losing one of their own.

Bel heard hushed murmuring as he noticed the folks staring long and hard at him, wondering if he was here to bring them more grief. But then, Bel saw Ella Desmond push through the crowd and stand before the big gray. She was dressed in a simple black dress with a black, netted veil atop her head. Bel touched his hand to his hat brim.

"Sorry I missed the funeral, ma'am," Bel greeted. "I got back as quick as I could."

"It's quite alright, Mr. Jensen," Desmond replied, gazing up at the young rider. "It...it's nice to see you again."

"Same here, ma'am."

The townsfolk began to go their separate ways, touching Ella Desmond lightly on the shoulder in consolation, or whispering a few kind words in her ear. She smiled briefly, nodding at their kind gestures.

Bel dropped the sacks of money at Desmond's feet. "It's all there. Ten thousand dollars."

She stared at the loot, disbelief in her eyes that it had been recovered, glancing back up at Bel. "What about...the thieves who stole it?"

"They won't be coming back," Bel replied matter-of-factly.
"Neither will the sheriff and the men that road with him."

"Oh. They were killed, too?"

"In a matter of speaking, ma'am. They were shot from ambush.
Saw their bodies on the ride back."

Desmond's brow furrowed. "But, I don't under..."

"I'm afraid," Bel explained, "to be the one to tell you this, Miss
Desmond, but Sheriff Thompson was the ramrod in this whole mess."

Her mouth opened in shock. "Oh, my word!"

"Thompson sent the Collier gang to this bank here, and was
going to buy out the owners when they went under. Pretty simple,
really."

"What was my father's involvement in all this?"

"Nothing at all. He...he was just in the wrong place at the wrong
time, I'm afraid."

Ella Desmond bowed her head, and when she looked back up,
tears were welling up in her eyes. "I...I don't know what to say...Bel.
You risked your life by taking on a job that you were under no

obligation to fulfill. Why?"

Bel gave a curt smile. "I learned a lot on my journey. I even faced my fears...and conquered them, I think."

Ella's face brightened with a wide, compassionate smile of her own. "Thank you, Bel Jensen. For everything."

"Just doing what I thought was right, ma'am."

"What will you do now? Will you stay?"

"I was thinking about it. But first, I need to go somewhere, and I was wondering if you'd like to come with me?"

"Where?"

Bel's features hardened into stone. "To face some old demons and pay my last respects."

"Yes, I'd like that very much, Bel."

Bel held out his hand to Ella Desmond and she took it, hauling the young woman up into the saddle behind him. Then he nudged his horse into a trot and headed down the street to the Desmond house to prepare for one last ride.

The wind blew across the short-grass country with an eerie song as Bel Jensen stood on the hill with Ella Desmond beside him, surveying the valley where Sanctuary once thrived.

Now, it was nothing but a ghost town. The buildings were rotted and wind-blasted, sitting silently on the flat. This time of the morning, people would be going about their business, coming into town to shop for supplies, or for a little conversation. But, no more. The town was dead.

How long had it been since Bel had been there? He thought back and figured it had to be around five years or so since he'd left. What had happened in those years that had killed this once thriving community?

Ella Desmond, clad in a denim riding outfit, curled her arm under Bel's as he directed his intense gaze toward the row of dead buildings. Bel couldn't get over how radiant she looked. The wind blew her hair across her ivory face, the sun shone brightly, accentuating her clear skin, magnifying the beautiful woman she was.

Bel tucked her arm tighter, bringing her just a bit closer as he saw her looking at him with concern in her eyes.

"Are you okay, Bel? You seem troubled?"

"I'm okay, Ella. It just seems strange that I come back to the place where I grew up, and it's gone. All gone."

Up the hill at the mission, they saw much of the same of what they saw of Sanctuary. The burned out timbers of the main house still stood, but the barn was in disrepair. The adobe mission itself was crumbling, with piles of wood and adobe bricks littered around the structure.

On the trip from Dry Springs, they'd talked at length about their childhoods. Bel had told Ella all about his troubled youth here at the mission and his friendships with Sister Katherine and Micah MacLean later on toward young adulthood.

He'd talked at length to her about his powers that he never knew he had, and how bad things seemed to happen whenever he blacked out. She'd listened intently, asking questions with a tone of gentleness, or reaching out to hold his hand while he talked of the sad times he'd experienced.

It brought Bel Jensen closer to Ella Desmond in those few days on the trail, than he ever thought possible with anyone else. With most people, Bel was usually quiet and reserved, but with Ella, he'd talked like they'd been old friends for years. It made him feel more alive and he chided himself for missing this aspect of his life after all this time.

Now the two of them, arm in arm, made their way toward the ruined adobe mission, and Bel spotted something behind the structure. The wind picked up, blowing dust from the front yard in large swirls, as they covered their eyes and walked behind the mission to see what was there.

Bel's stomach went sick as he saw the headstones all in a row in the small patch of green grass. They were all there; Sister Mary, Sister Lupe, Father Garcia and eleven smaller stones for the children that had been there at the time of the fire. But...

His and Ella's mouths opened in shock as they spotted his name on the last marker.

A horse whinnied and Bel turned around, trying to see through the haze of brown grit churned up by the blowing gust of wind. The outline of a figure was coming from the front of the mission, making its way through the brown, cloudy wall.

The figure was dressed all in black with its face covered. No, it couldn't be, Bel gaped. It couldn't be the Grim Reaper, like the one that had come for Micah MacLean.

Bel unholstered his gun and pointed it at the approaching figure.

"Bel, who is it?" Ella asked.

"I...I don't know."

The black wraith came to stand about five feet from Bel and Ella. Bel snapped back the hammer on his Colt, Ella braced directly behind him. "Who are you?" he demanded. "A ghost from the past? You're not taking us like you took my friend Micah!"

The wind seemed to die down, and it took a few moments for the dust to settle. The figure reached up slowly to pull the dark hood back. Then it spoke.

"Bel? Is that you?"

"What?"

Bel saw the auburn hair and the kind, gentle features that belonged to a woman he hadn't seen in ten years. Her face had a few more wrinkles around the eyes, but she looked almost exactly as he remembered her. He didn't know how or why, but he was staring at Sister Katherine.

Bel's eyes widened in surprise, and a huge smile played across his face. He went forward to stand in front of Katherine, holstering his gun and gripping her shoulders in each of his hands.

"I...I almost can't believe it's you, Sister Katherine!" Bel stammered, excitement overwhelming him.

"Oh, Lord God, you're alive, Bel Jensen," Katherine gushed. Then she turned serious and looked deep into Bel's eyes. "It's...a miracle! I...I thought you'd died with the rest of them."

Then Bel couldn't help but pull the lady into his arms, and they stood there for the next few minutes, just embracing, rocking back and forth. The tears started to come, and as they pulled back, Bel chuckled, wiping his eyes. He turned to Ella.

"Ella, this is the nun I told you about---Sister Katherine. She treated me so very nicely while I was here. Sister, this is my friend, Ella Desmond."

The two women hugged like they were old friends. Then Bel put his arm around Katherine, and he felt like the solemn little boy she had befriended all those years ago.

"Sister, what happened to you?" Bel asked. "They said you were sent away, and I never heard from you again. You never said goodbye or anything. I kinda figured Sister Mary had something to do with it."

She closed her eyes momentarily, then gazed at Bel. "Bel, you must believe me that I didn't want to go. Sister Mary pressured Father Garcia to have me re-assigned. He finally relented. I was sent to St. Louis. They thought my feeling and attention for you had clouded my judgment, so I wasn't allowed to send you any letters to explain." She clasped Bel's hand in hers. "I...was in pain for having to leave the mission. I never wanted any of it to happen, but I had to remember I was doing the Lord's bidding. So, after a while I accepted it, and went on with my life. Will you forgive me, Bel?"

Bel patted Katherine's hand. "I never blamed you, Sister Katherine. They were just circumstances that were out of our control."

The three of them walked inside the mission and sat down in one of the stone pews. There were at least a dozen pews on each side of the building with a long walkway that led up a few steps to the altar. All the ornate marble sculptures of the Virgin Mary and saints had crumbled or been disfigured. Even the simple wooden cross with a stone figure of Jesus was missing part of the head and an arm.

Ella Desmond asked, "Sister, what brought you out here? Bel was shocked to see that the town had died out."

"Sanctuary," Katherine said with a touch of sadness. "When I heard about the fire, they'd said there were no survivors. It was on that same night that the town marshal was found dead behind his office." When she mentioned Micah MacLean, Bel tensed up. "I don't know, after those two horrible accidents, the town never recovered."

"Why? What happened?" Ella asked.

"People started to move out farther west, the ranch land in the area seemed to go bad, streams dried up. It was like those two events placed a black cloud over the entire valley. The town just...died. For five years now on the anniversary of the fire, I've been coming out to pay my respects."

Bel couldn't help but shake his head in dismay as he listened to Sister Katherine's story.

"What's wrong, Bel?" Katherine asked.

"I started the fire by accident, Sister Katherine. It was one of my blackouts. It took me all these years to figure it all out. I was responsible for killing all those children, Sister Lupe and Sister Mary, and Father Garcia. All of them! It's my fault!"

Ella Desmond knew most of the story behind Bel's troubled past, and he knew she felt his pain from him telling her his life while they were on the trail. Bel could tell Sister Katherine took in the admission with a sense of empathy, and noticed she remained calm.

"You had no control over it, Bel," Katherine assured him. "There was nothing you could have done. Like you said, the circumstances were out of your control."

"But, figure it out I did," Bel said. "It all came to me in a revelation. I now know what I am and who I am. Everything is so clear."

Bel hesitated, looking between Ella and Sister Katherine. Ella nodded to him with the utmost understanding.

"What is it, Bel?" Katherine pleaded.

"I am fear," Bel stated.

He'd not even told this to Ella, and both women had perplexed looks on their faces. Bel cracked a half-smile at their lack of understanding. "*I...AM...FEAR,*" Bel said slowly. "In the flesh."

"How can that be?" Ella wondered.

"Ella, you know I've already told you that somehow, some way I can transform myself into people's worst fears. I know it sounds crazy..." He looked to Sister Katherine. "But, that's been my curse all these years. I can see into people's thoughts, I can manifest their fears into reality. I become their worst nightmares."

"My friend Micah was afraid of the image of the Grim Reaper; a group of rustlers were petrified of Indians; the Collier gang had fears ranging from a famous lawman, to being drowned, to a visage of Satan, to some horrific monstrosity that I can't even begin to explain. And Sister Mary didn't like bees. In the end, it killed her, along with so many others."

Sister Katherine crossed herself. "Were you...born...of the devil...?"

"Like Sister Mary thought?" Bel finished for her. "No, I don't think so. The night of that terrible storm, there was torrential rain, peals and peals of thunder and huge bursts of lightning. Those acts of nature in themselves can be quite frightening to any normal person.

"In some freak way, these tremendous forces caused a powerful convergence of energy into one, single, solitary spot. In essence, it created fear in the form of---Me. That's why I was completely dry that night. I came into being on the front porch of the main house. In a sense you could say I was born from the loins of Mother Nature herself."

"Why wouldn't you have appeared as a baby?" Katherine asked.

"I don't know if I can explain that," Bel said. "Everyone has fear in them, but babies can't *tell* you what they fear. Maybe I was manifested around the age when children consciously know fear and what they're afraid of. But, I'll never be sure."

Sister Katherine was visibly overwhelmed by what she was hearing, as was Ella. The nun once again reached out to take hold of Bel's hand. "But, you were a good boy, Bel," she said. "You've obviously grown up to be a good man. And I think you kept your promise to me...not using your special power for evil."

"Didn't you mention something about 'The Figure'?" Ella asked.

"Unfortunately," Bel continued, "there were two sides to the fear power. The Figure was the part of me that controlled my actions

when I had the blackouts. It was the piece of my personality that

reveled in the anxieties of men, women and children. It basically

controlled me during those times I was in duress."

"What about now?" Katherine wondered. "Will you have these

blackouts again?"

"I...feel...different," Bel said, "now that I know the truth. It could

be that maybe The Figure is in a state of hibernation. But, then

again, maybe not. I guess only time will tell."

"What will you do now?" Katherine asked.

"I want to settle down," Bel stated. He gazed lovingly at Ella

Desmond, who smiled shyly at the young man. "And Dry Springs

seems like a good place to start."

"You should come out that way, Sister Katherine," Ella offered.

"You'd be very welcome. In fact, I think the town council was talking

about finally putting up a church."

"I should be able to persuade Father O'Meara back in St. Louis

that Dry Springs would be a perfect place to have me continue my

work. Maybe even continue the work Sister Mary and I started here?"

"I would be glad to help," Bel said.

"And I would be very happy to have you, Bel," Sister Katherine said.

After Sister Katherine put flowers on the graves behind the mission, and saying a little prayer, the trio walked back toward the ruins of the main house and the front yard, preparing to depart. They mounted their horses, and as one looked back toward the adobe mission.

"Bel," Ella started, "what if The Figure awakens from your consciousness? Hopefully your blackouts are behind you, but what if they aren't? What if He decides that He wants to be the sole resident of your personality? What then?"

Bel looked at Katherine and Ella Desmond, glancing back at the mission. "I don't know what the future might bring for me, Ella. Hopefully the worst is behind me." His blue eyes narrowed into hard slits. "What I do know is that I'll live my life to the fullest from now on. I'll meet any challenges head on, face my fears...and conquer them." Then he smiled warmly. "Just like your father would have done."

With that, the two ladies kicked their horses into a trot and Bel prepared to follow behind them. He turned his big gray to stare intently at the ruined house.

He might have been mistaken, but the way the sun and shadows were hitting the burned-out structure, Bel thought he saw dark phantoms standing amid the rubble watching him go.

He hoped they could rest in peace now. Bel knew that he would rest a bit easier now.

He touched the brim of his hat in solemn acknowledgment, turning to catch up with the women, riding off with thoughts of a new and brighter tomorrow...and being at peace with himself.

www.ingramcontent.com/pod-product-compliance
Lightning Source LLC
Chambersburg PA
CBHW020438180626
46812CB00003B/1291